THE POSTMASTER OF TREBLINKA

A History Mystery Novella

GABRIEL FARAGO

This book is brought to you by Bear & King Publishing.

Publishing & Marketing Consultant: Lama Jabr
Website: https://xanapublishingandmarketing.com/
Sydney, Australia

First published 2022 © Gabriel Farago

ISBN 978-0-9876283-4-3

Sign up for the author's New Releases mailing list and get a free copy of *The Forgotten Painting** novella to find out where it all began ...

https://gabrielfarago.com.au/free-download-forgotten-painting/

* I'm delighted to tell you that *The Forgotten Painting* has just received two major literary awards in the US. It was awarded the Gold Medal by Readers' Favorite in the Short Stories and Novellas category and was named the 'Outstanding Novella' of 2018 by the Independent Author Network (IAN) Book of the Year Awards.

Also by Gabriel Farago

Dear reader,

Before you start reading, just a few words about the novella as a literary genre:

The novella made its first appearance in the early Renaissance, especially in Italy and France. Giovanni Boccaccio's *The Decameron* (1349), and *Heptaméron* (1558–1559), penned by French queen Marguerite de Navarre and modelled on *The Decameron*, were the trailblazers. However, it wasn't until the late eighteenth and early nineteenth centuries that the novella took shape as the literary genre we know today.

Robert Silverberg in *Sailing to Byzantium* (2000) describes the novella as *'one of the richest and most rewarding of literary forms ... it allows for more extended development of theme and character than does the short story, without making the elaborate structural demands of the full-length book. Thus it provides an intense, detailed exploration of its subject, providing to some degree both the concentrated focus of the short story and the broad scope of the novel.'*

The Postmaster of Treblinka is a novella and as such it is, of course, much shorter than my novels, but without losing focus or scope. That was one of the reasons I chose this genre as the vehicle to explore certain hidden corners of Jack Rogan's life, and reveal a little more about his background and character.

AUTHOR'S NOTE

As *The Jack Rogan Mysteries Series* has just reached another milestone, with seven books and now three novellas – a body of work that now encompasses more than 3500 paperback pages – a brief explanation of the idea behind this novella is warranted.

While all the books in the series stand alone and can be read as such, all of them are also interrelated, and readers familiar with all the books, who have perhaps read them in chronological order, will have a much more satisfying reading experience and get a great deal more out of the series generally.

The idea behind the novellas is straightforward and clear: they are intended to further enhance that reading experience by 'branching out' and exploring aspects of Jack Rogan's life and the lives of other key characters, which in the context of the main novels just isn't possible.

The best way to illustrate this is to consider the series as a large tree with many branches. The novels in the series are the trunk and the main branches. The novellas are smaller branches that give the tree its shape, character and charm.

Encouraged by the reception of the first novella, *The Forgotten Painting* (2016), which has won two major literary awards, I soon turned my mind to another one, *The Kimberley Secret*, released in 2018. Because I enjoy a close relationship with many of my readers and listen to their suggestions and requests, I used this novella to explore aspects of Jack Rogan's earlier life. His childhood, his family; in short, the building blocks of his character and personality my readers have grown to love.

That said, there was another important reason behind releasing the novellas: to introduce new readers to the series and showcase my writing.

The idea behind this third novella is no different, but the way I have approached the subject matter requires some explanation.

In essence, the storyline reaches back to *The Forgotten Painting* and follows the life of David Herzl, the World War II master forger of

Warsaw. To do this in a meaningful way, I have introduced some 'flashback' material taken from the first novella and a number of other books in the series, to provide a direct link to the characters and the storylines featured there.

To do this effectively without tedious repetitions is never easy, and I have addressed this issue by using several 'flashback' chapters or scenes taken directly from *The Forgotten Painting*. Readers familiar with that novella will be reminded of what occurred then, and new readers who read the novella as a standalone book, will be assisted in following the plot.

In the end, what really matters here is the quality of the reading experience. Hopefully, *The Postmaster of Treblinka* will become another exciting branch of the tree, to entertain you and provide further insights into the lives and tribulations of the main characters featured in the series.

I hope you enjoy the journey as much as I did!

Gabriel Farago
Leura, Blue Mountains; Australia
1 February 2022

CONTENTS

"Hope is the thing with feathers
That perches in the soul
And sings the tune without the words
And never stops at all."
— **Emily Dickinson**

Old Jewish Cemetery, Prague: 1 August 2019

It was oppressively hot and raining, and a dense fog drifted across the river like a shroud. *Different from last time*, thought Jack as he remembered the heavy snow and icy wind he'd had to brave on his way to the cemetery two years earlier.

Just like on the previous occasion, Jack had given himself plenty of time to reach his destination, as he didn't want to be late and keep Avigdor Stein waiting. The Old Jewish Cemetery in Prague's crowded Jewish Quarter in the middle of town, with its twelve thousand headstones – many of them broken and covered in moss and ivy – dated back to the fifteenth century. Because Jewish customs strictly forbid the removal of graves, and due to limited space in a cemetery that had outgrown its needs centuries ago, it's estimated that more than a hundred thousand bodies had been buried there through the ages – in some places stacked ten deep on top of one another.

During the Nazi occupation, all traces of Jewish culture, including synagogues and cemeteries, were systematically erased in the occupied countries, with relentless German efficiency. The reason the Old Jewish Cemetery and the Jewish Museum, with its thousands of precious historical artefacts, were spared by the Nazis was due to a dark, sinister plan: the establishment of an 'Extinct Race Museum' in Prague. The exhibits on display in this museum would tell future generations the story of an extinct culture and race, wiped out by superior Aryans.

Jack stopped at the walled entrance and smiled. This time, he knew exactly where he had to go. Just like before, Stein had suggested they meet at the grave of Judah Loew ben Bazalel, the enigmatic, sixteenth-century rabbi of Prague, who had created the most famous golem narrative handed down through the ages.

As Jack walked along the solemn rows of graves towards the ornate sand-coloured headstone engraved with a lion, he could see Stein standing next to it. Wearing a long black coat and black hat, the curator of the Jewish Museum looked like a Hebrew sentinel guarding the

1

domain of the dead. Most befitting for one of the most knowledgeable scholars of European twentieth-century Jewish history, thought Jack as he waved.

'We meet again,' said Stein, extending his hand, his long white beard, sidelocks and prominent nose giving him an almost biblical look.

'And just like last time, we meet at the grave of Rabbi Loew, just as you requested,' said Jack.

'We do. And do you remember what Rabbi Loew – also known as the Maharal of Prague – was famous for?'

'Of course. According to legend, the Maharal created a golem out of clay taken from the banks of the Vltava River—'

'And brought it to life,' interjected Stein, 'by using ancient Hebrew rituals and incantations to defend the Prague ghetto from pogroms.'

'We had a very similar conversation last time we met,' said Jack, smiling.

'We did. And can you still remember what a golem is?'

'I do. A golem is an anthropomorphic – a being in human form – created entirely from inanimate matter, like clay or mud.'

'Which according to Jewish folklore is a changeable metaphor with endless symbolism. It can be a Jew, or gentile, man or woman. It can signify war, isolation, even despair, but also hope, generosity and compassion,' said Stein.

'And friendship?' asked Jack.

'Oh yes, that too, of course.'

'Good,' said Jack. 'In a way, friendship is the reason I wanted to meet with you again. This is all about a remarkable friendship that has transcended a horrendous murder, unspeakable atrocities of war, and the brutality of man.'

Jack reached into his pocket, pulled out an envelope, and handed it to Stein. 'This is the final stage of a letter's long journey that began in the infamous Ipatiev House in Yekaterinburg in 1918. From there, the journey took the letter to Treblinka, the Nazi death camp, before finally reaching the home of Countess Bezukhova in France in 1943.'

'Ah. The letter written by Empress Alexandra, the last tsarina, the day before she and her entire family were murdered by the Bolsheviks,' said Stein. He opened the envelope and took out a sheet of paper, his fingers trembling. '*It is!*' he exclaimed, his voice quivering with emotion. 'The original?'

'Yes. For the museum. I believe this is where it belongs. After all, the only reason it made it to its destination twenty-five years after it was written, was because of the ingenuity and courage of David Herzl.'

'The Postmaster of Treblinka,' said Stein.

'Correct. And the loyalty of Pavel Ustinov.'

'The Golem of Treblinka. And the rest of this extraordinary journey is all in your book, *The Lost Symphony*,' said Stein. 'I read it. I also saw the hand-over ceremony on TV of Kazanskaya Bogomater, the holy icon, in the Alexander Nevsky Cathedral in Yekaterinburg. You sat in the front row facing the altar between Abbot Serapion and Patriarch Nicodemus, the Primate of the Russian Orthodox Church. And, of course, the pope was there too. A historic occasion indeed. And it was you who walked up to the altar and placed the holy icon on its pedestal after the Patriarch had handed it to you. A great honour. Very moving.'

'You have an excellent memory. But none of that would have been possible without your help,' said Jack, 'and for that I will be forever in your debt.'

'You were following your breadcrumbs of destiny,' said Stein. 'Perhaps all of us did.'

'Perhaps. And those breadcrumbs bring me here this morning. Empress Alexandra's letter that I found in the music box left to me by my great-aunt, Madame Petrova, belongs right here, in this museum. This must be its final resting place. Just like the holy icon had to be returned to where it belongs, and *Mat' Rossiya* – Tchaikovsky's lost symphony – had to be returned to St Petersburg and given to the Russian people.'

'This is an act of great generosity,' said Stein. 'I know what this letter must mean to you.'

'We cannot own history. I believe it belongs to this place here.' Jack pointed to the countless rows of silent graves. 'Among the "well of souls with thousands of voices", I think you called it last time we met, who help you unlock the secrets of ancient manuscripts and letters penned a long time ago.'

'Speaking of letters penned a long time ago,' said Stein, grinning, 'I have something for you I know you will find interesting. No, more than that. You will find *irresistible.*'

'How intriguing. What is it?'

'A troubling mystery that has been on my mind for years. It is mentioned in Herzl's diary.'

'The Postmaster of Treblinka again?'

'Yes. It's a mystery that has to be investigated, and I believe you are the one to do just that.'

'Why me?'

'Because of who you are. You are a man of destiny. And this mystery is all about destiny.'

'Can you tell me more?'

'Of course. Come, let's go into the museum and I'll tell you all you need to know.'

As Jack followed Stein up the creaking stairs to his study above the museum, he could feel the fine hairs on the back of his neck beginning to tingle. It was a familiar premonition that rarely let him down, and usually meant a new adventure or challenge was hurtling towards him out of the toolbox of destiny.

Arquà Petrarca, Veneto region near Padua: September 1923

Covered in sweat and trying in vain to go to sleep, Isabella tossed and turned restlessly in her bed. It had been an unusually hot day and the still, oppressive air hovered like a stifling blanket over the silent village. The refreshing evening breeze that usually blew in from the Adriatic to the east had failed to arrive, to cool the parched land dreaming of autumn and longing for elusive rain.

Suddenly, she heard strange music drifting across the fields from the village below. The mesmerising beat of drums and jangle of tambourines was soon joined by the seductive sound of violins and the mournful cry of a duduk, conjuring up fleeting images of distant lands and whirling dervishes honouring their god.

Isabella got out of bed and walked out onto the balcony overlooking the manicured gardens of the stately villa that had been the home of the Alberti family – prominent landed gentry of the district – for centuries. It was cooler outside, but the marble floor was still warm, making the soles of her bare feet tingle. As she looked across the fields, she could see a fire burning just outside the village and dark shapes moving to the spellbinding rhythm of the drums, sending crazy shadows dancing along the walls of the little cemetery.

The gypsies. Of course! she thought and quickly got dressed. A group of gypsies had arrived with their horse-drawn wagons the day before and set up camp just outside the village. They came every year as a welcome addition to the workforce to help with the harvest, which had been part of village life for a long time.

Unable to resist the siren call of the music, Isabella tiptoed past her father's bedroom and then down the stairs to the silent corridor leading to the back door. There she paused, put on her shoes and opened the door. Taking a deep breath she looked around, and then quickly stepped outside.

Guided by the ghostly light of a full moon that seemed to suck the colour out of the sleeping landscape, Isabella hurried across the lush fields towards the village and followed the stirring music, making her

5

blood boil and her cheeks glow with excitement and the lure of the unknown.

The colourful wagons had been arranged in a semicircle facing a fire. The musicians, all men, sat under a large tree in the shadows, while several young women were dancing around the fire – ignoring the children trying to do the same – watched by a group of old men smoking pipes and drinking homemade grappa.

Mesmerised by the spectacle, so different from village life ruled by the Church and age-old, rigid traditions, Isabella stood behind a hedge – watching – not daring to come closer. She was straining her neck to see better, when she heard a voice from behind.

'You don't have to hide, you know,' said the voice softly. 'Visitors are always welcome.'

Isabella spun around, her heart missing a beat, and looked straight into the eyes of a young man standing in the shadows behind her. His eyes – dark and shiny – radiated kindness, but also danger, and seemed to look straight through her.

'I am Django,' said the young man, 'and that's my family over there.'

'I'm Isabella, I live in the house up on the hill.'

'I saw you crossing the fields,' continued the young man, his soft voice melodious, with a seductive edge and unfamiliar accent hinting at a foreign origin. 'So, what will it be? Are we just going to stand here and watch, or would you like to meet my family? I can assure you that they would be delighted to make your acquaintance.'

'Let's go and meet them,' said Isabella, surprising herself with the answer.

Without saying another word, Django took Isabella by the hand and together they walked into the circle of light.

By the time Isabella tiptoed back to her room, it was well past three am. Lying on her bed – hot and sweaty after dancing with the women by the fire – she watched the shafts of moonlight reach through the open windows like fingers of a gentle giant.

Meeting Django and his exotic family appeared like a dream, and the stirring music like a strange wakeup call igniting unsettling feelings and desires in her she had never encountered before. Slowly, she ran the tips of her fingers along her right cheek where Django had briefly kissed her on the way back to the house. She could still feel the touch of his hot lips, and his muscular body pressing against hers before they parted on a promise to meet again the next night.

But most unsettling by far, were the words of the old woman who had read her palm: 'You will have two sons,' she heard the woman say, her rasping voice sounding otherworldly. 'One of them will rise to high office, the other ...' Instead of completing the sentence, the woman had stared at her with sad eyes and let go of her hand, the look in those eyes sending a cold shiver of fear racing down Isabella's spine.

Isabella closed her eyes, trying in vain to banish the unnerving encounter with the old woman, and tried to go to sleep, but the haunting look of sadness in the old woman's eyes wouldn't go away. Only when Isabella turned her mind to Django, the most handsome young man she had ever seen in her young life, did the disturbing image begin to recede.

The gypsies stayed in the village for three weeks. Isabella and Django met almost every day. Sometimes in the fields – brushing against each other as they helped with the harvest and exchanging secret looks of longing and desire – sometimes in the shade under a tree while sharing a meal break with the others. However, most precious of all was their time together late at night when they met at their secret place in the bushes behind the house, to make love until the first rays of the morning sun melted the darkness and Isabella had to return to her room before the household stirred, and the squawking peacocks in the garden announced the beginning of a new day.

Arquà Petrarca: one year later, September 1924

The gypsies had just arrived to help with the harvest, as they did every year.

Padre Angelis, the village priest, walked up to Menowin Santi, Django's father, who was the voivode of the clan. Elected for life, the voivode was the chieftain of the Albanian gypsy band that arrived in the village each autumn. The priest had known Santi for years and had acted as go-between and negotiator between the gypsies and the villagers, especially when it came to ironing out tensions, which did arise from time to time.

'Alberti wants to see you,' said Angelis as he helped Santi secure one of the wagons in the camp that was being set up.

'Oh? Is there a problem?' asked Santi, carefully watching the padre.

Angelis shrugged.

'I take that as a yes.' Santi finished tying a knot. 'Let's go. Alberti doesn't like to be kept waiting.'

Claudio Alberti was an imposing man. Tall, in his late thirties with an aristocratic bearing that radiated authority, he was the head of a family that had lived in the Veneto region for centuries and had accumulated huge wealth. With wealth came influence and power, and Alberti knew how to use both. Isabella's mother had died in childbirth, and Isabella was his only child and the apple of his eye. The meeting he had arranged was all about her and her future, and by implication the future of the family.

'We have known each other for a long time, Menowin,' said Alberti after Santi and Angelis had been admitted into his study on the ground floor overlooking the garden.

'We have,' said Santi, wondering where this was heading.

'You have always been trustworthy and a man of your word. You have the respect of your people, and they listen to you and value your judgement and counsel.'

'Thank you,' said Santi, beginning to feel uneasy.

'What I'm about to tell you must remain strictly between us three.

You will see why in a moment. Lives depend on it.'

Santi nodded.

Alberti picked up a bell on his desk and rang it. Moments later, a maid entered carrying a baby in her arms. Without saying a word, she handed the baby to Alberti and left the room.

'Come over here, Menowin, and meet your grandson. *Our* grandson,' said Alberti.

'I ... I don't understand,' stammered Santi, looking incredulous, his head spinning.

'You will in a moment. Last year, Isabella and your son, Django, met during the harvest. Two teenagers attracted to each other. They became lovers, and this is the result. Understandable and natural. I didn't see it coming, and I'm sure neither did you.'

'I had no idea!'

'Just as I thought. Do you want to hold him?'

'Yes, please.'

Alberti handed the baby to Santi. 'A beautiful child, wouldn't you say?'

'Gorgeous.'

'Yes, but at the same time, a big problem. For me and my family, and especially for Isabella.'

'I don't follow.'

'Then let me explain,' said Padre Angelis, stepping in.

'A seventeen-year-old girl, the heir to the Alberti fortune, promised in marriage to the son of a prominent neighbour ... now, mother to an illegitimate child.' Angelis looked at Santi and raised an eyebrow. 'Do you follow now?'

'Yes, yes, of course. Where is Isabella?'

'At our summer residence in Venice. She gave birth there, sheltered from prying eyes and loose tongues. I sent her there as soon as her pregnancy became obvious. This entire matter has to remain a secret; you do understand, don't you?'

'Yes, but ...' Santi held up the baby, 'what about the child?'

'We believe there is a solution,' said Angelis.

'What kind of solution?'

'I'll tell you,' said Alberti, pleased by the way the conversation was turning to the subject that was foremost on his mind.

During the next half hour, Alberti, an experienced tactician and negotiator, calmly explained what he saw as a solution to the problem.

'So, what do you say, Menowin?' asked Alberti, watching Santi carefully.

'I have to think about it and discuss it with the family.'

'Understandable. But please keep in mind that this entire matter has to remain a secret.' Alberti held up his hand. 'I am a generous man ...'

'We are used to secrets. That's the only way we have been able to survive.'

'How true,' said Angelis.

'I will give you my answer in the morning,' said Santi. He handed the baby back to Alberti, took a bow and left.

Early the next morning, Esmeralda Santi, Django's mother, presented herself at the Alberti residence. Alberti looked at the striking woman coming towards him with interest.

'I am Esmeralda Santi, the phuri dai of our clan,' said the woman. 'I am also Menowin's wife and the mother of Django.'

'Thank you for coming,' said Alberti and pointed to a chair facing his desk. 'Please take a seat. May I ask, what is a phuri dai?'

'The phuri dai is a senior woman of the clan who is responsible for the welfare of the women and children. It's an age-old tradition.'

'I see. A very good one, no doubt. And you are here in that capacity?'

'Yes, and also as the mother of Django, the father of the child. May I see the baby?'

'Of course,' said Alberti and rang the bell. Moments later, the maid entered and handed the baby to Esmeralda. For a while, Esmeralda just looked dreamily at the baby in her arms and smiled. Then she looked at Alberti, watching her carefully.

'My husband promised to give you his answer today,' she said. 'The clan has discussed the matter and made a decision—'

'And?'

'We will do as you ask. The child will become part of our family and grow up as a member of the clan. He will be given the name Anibal, which means graced by God. The child will be under my personal care and protection, and you can rest assured that your secret will be safe with us.'

'I am grateful,' said Alberti, relieved. 'You will not regret this—'

'*Regret?*' said Esmeralda, surprised. 'Why should I ever regret this decision?' She looked at the sleeping baby in her arms. 'You have given me a treasure.'

'I'm glad you see it that way.'

'May I ask you a question?'

'Of course.'

'How can you, and especially Isabella, the mother, contemplate this? How can you bear parting with this child? Please help me understand.'

Alberti pointed to the family crest on the wall behind his desk. 'The path of duty can be painful,' he said with sadness in his voice.

'You hear the voice of duty, not of love,' said Esmeralda and stood up. 'I only hear the voice of love. Worldly possessions come and go, but love is eternal. This child will always be loved, whatever happens. That, I promise you.'

Palazzo da Baggio, Venice: 5 August 2019

Jack sat on the terrace of the palazzo he now called home, overlooking the Grand Canal and surrounded by ancient edifices rising out of the lagoon like sentinels guarding secrets of a glorious past. It was his 'new' favourite place where he did some of his most creative thinking, having replaced the conservatory at the Kuragin chateau just outside Paris, with its exotic indoor palms and the stunning view across the frozen pond in winter, watched over by snow-covered pine trees looking like bearded old men in fur coats. It was early in the morning, and the palazzos competing for memories on the opposite side were still shrouded in mist, putting a cottonwool dampener on the cacophony of sound rising from the canal, buzzing with morning traffic.

Stein had been right; Jack found the troubling mystery challenge the rabbi had thrown him irresistible. He was instantly hooked. Following his breadcrumbs of destiny, he had gone straight to Budapest to talk to Sandor Kun, who had donated his father's diary to the Jewish Museum in Prague. As the fascinating mystery was linked to the Postmaster of Treblinka, starting with his son seemed logical.

'How was Budapest?' asked Countess Kuragin. 'You came in late.' She walked over to Jack and ran her fingers playfully through his hair, the gesture of natural affection reminding him of Lorenza. 'Coffee?'

'Yes, please.' Jack pointed to his notes on the table in front of him. 'I'm finally beginning to make some sense of all this; *what a story*! And it all started with one courageous man who saw beauty among unspeakable evil, used a unique talent to stay alive, and overcame the unthinkable through love and without losing his humanity. Amazing, don't you think?'

'You and your stories. I don't know how they find you,' said the countess, shaking her head.

'Neither do I, but somehow they do.' Jack held up a piece of paper. 'This one began with a diary entry Stein showed me when I visited him in Prague last week to give him Empress Alexandra's letter for his museum—'

'The one you found in Madame Petrova's music box that started your Russian adventure?'

'Yes, and now this. Another challenge, a fascinating one. Come, have a look at this.' Jack pointed to the top right-hand corner of the piece of paper in his hand.

'What's that?'

'A signature.'

'Seriously? It looks like a tiny heart and a star.'

'It is. The Star of David.'

'And that's a signature?'

'It sure is. The signature of a brave man. A very talented one. David Herzl, a painter and master forger who dared to look evil in the eye and managed to stare it down. The Star of David stands for David, of course, and the heart for Herzl, which means little heart in German.'

'The same David Herzl who painted the Monet forgery that caused such a fuss when the original painting was auctioned in London?'

'Yes. The Emil Fuchs affair, but David Herzl's story starts much earlier, in the Warsaw Ghetto—'

'You wrote about that in your novella, *The Forgotten Painting*, right?'

'I did. And little did I know then that I would encounter Herzl again. First, in connection with Alexandra's letter to Countess Bezukhova and its extraordinary delivery twenty-five years after it had been written, and now this.'

'Strange how all these stories are interconnected, don't you think?'

'Absolutely. That's the really fascinating thing about all this.'

Jack looked dreamily across the canal to the facades of the palazzos emerging from the mist, banished by the rays of the morning sun heralding a new day. It was like a curtain being drawn, revealing glimpses of a hidden past.

'Tristan has an explanation for this, you know. He believes it's all about unfinished business that has to be resolved before the soul can find peace,' said Jack. 'He can hear voices—'

'You are talking about me?' said Tristan, who had overheard the remark as he walked out onto the terrace.

'You can't keep anything from this guy,' said Jack, rolling his eyes.

'You must have heard the whisper of angels,' teased the countess.

'Is that it?'

'Perhaps. All I can tell you is they were whispering about some mystery Jack has got himself entangled in – *again*.' Tristan raised an eyebrow, turned to Jack and looked at him sternly. 'Could you perhaps help us with that, Jack?'

'Sure. Herzl's story began in the Warsaw Ghetto, remember?'

'Yes, when he painted *Little Sparrow in the Garden* for Berenger Krakowski and tricked the Germans,' said Tristan.

'Correct, and like all good stories, one must start at the beginning. You of all people know that. Before I can tell you about the Postmaster of Treblinka and his Ballroom of Hope, you must first meet the man in the Warsaw Ghetto in 1942, and get to know him and understand how his mind works, and what makes him tick.'

'Ballroom of Hope?' said the countess. 'Intriguing. I'll get some coffee and you can tell us all about it. Are you ready for this, Tristan?'

'I think you should bring a few fresh pastries with the coffee. I have a feeling we'll be here for a while.'

'Good idea.'

Warsaw Ghetto: August 1942

By August 1942, the mass deportations from Warsaw were in full swing. As part of the wider 'Operation Reinhard', *Grossaktion Warschau* had only one aim: to deport thousands of Jews from the ghetto to Treblinka for extermination. Between 23 July and 21 September 1942, some three hundred thousand ghetto residents were sent to the death camps.

Berenger Krakowski walked over to the window and looked down into the street below. 'Look at them,' he said, watching another column of several hundred march silently towards the Umschlagplatz on Stawki Street, the notorious collection point. There, herded together like cattle, they would wait for the arrival of the trains.

'What are we going to do, Berenger?' asked Ruth, his wife. 'They are coming closer; it will be our turn any time now.'

'I spoke to Mandel again yesterday,' said Krakowski. Emanuel Mandel was a Jewish ghetto policeman working for the SS, and was helping the Germans to keep order in the crowded ghetto. Krakowski had given violin lessons to Mandel's daughter and was on reasonably good terms with him. He had fostered the relationship and used it as a source of valuable intelligence of what was happening in the ghetto. Being one step ahead of the SS could make the difference between life and death.

'What about?' said Ruth.

'The Germans are looking for paintings, especially impressionists …'

'Why?'

'Not sure, but Mandel seems to think that he can prevent our deportation if we can come up with something.'

'The Monet?'

'It's all we have left; we've sold everything else, except for the violin.'

'No, Berenger! You can't do that!'

'If the painting can save us, why not? I've taken it to Herzl.'

'Why?'

'To make us a copy. If we give them the painting, at least we'll have something to remind us ...'

Ruth walked over to her husband and put her arms around him. 'You are a good man, Berenger,' she said and kissed him on the cheek. 'Do what's best for us.'

'Always.'

David Herzl was a talented painter, but in the ghetto he was known as a master forger. Krakowski and Herzl were close friends, and when Krakowski had told him that he was thinking of giving his Monet to the Germans, to avoid transportation, Herzl offered to copy it for him.

Krakowski walked into Herzl's 'studio' hidden at the back of a damp cellar. 'How's it going?' he asked.

'See for yourself.' Herzl pointed to his easel.

'Incredible,' said Krakowski. The painting was almost finished. 'I can't tell them apart. I don't know how you do it, David, it's perfect.'

Herzl smiled. 'I can't create, but I can copy,' said Herzl, slapping his friend on the back.

'Mandel came around again today. He wants to arrange something for tomorrow, if possible. About the painting, I mean.'

'What?'

'A sale.'

'A sale? What do you mean?'

'Apparently, the SS want to bring someone over, some big shot from Berlin who wants to buy original paintings here in the ghetto. He's especially interested in impressionists.'

'*Buy*, you say? How weird.'

'That's what I thought. But who are we to question the Germans, eh? They are all mad, right?'

'You can collect the painting in the morning; I'll be finished by then. I'll keep the copy for you here until you're ready. I'll even frame it for you.'

'Thank you, my friend. Perhaps one day I can do something for you in return. I'll let Mandel know.'

Herzl worked through the night to finish the painting. Finally satisfied, he stood back and smiled. It was one of the best copies he had ever made. Exhausted, he lay down on his bunk next to the easel to get some sleep. He closed his eyes, but the much-needed sleep wouldn't come. Instead, Monet's *Little Sparrow in the Garden* began to whisper to him, seductively suggesting something daring. Covered in sweat, Herzl tossed and turned restlessly in his bunk, and tried to put the crazy idea out of his mind, but it wouldn't go away. Finally, he sat up and lit a candle. *Why not?* he thought. *It's good enough. They'll never notice the difference, those barbarians!*

Feeling better for having made a decision, Herzl walked over to the original painting, took it off the wall and began to carefully pull the frame apart.

Warsaw Ghetto: the 'sale', August 1942

The convertible Mercedes pulled up in front of Krakowski's dilapidated apartment block at precisely noon the next day. The driver jumped out of the car and opened the back door for the SS major and his young guest.

'Here we are, Herr Fuchs,' said the major and got out of the car.

Mandel was waiting nervously at the entrance, cap in hand, and watched the major come strutting towards him. 'Is everything ready?' demanded the major.

'*Jawohl*, Herr Sturmbannfuehrer,' said Mandel, standing to attention. 'First floor.'

'Show us the way.'

'*Jawohl*, Herr Sturmbannfuehrer.'

Wearing his best – and only – suit, Krakowski was waiting in his tiny, sparsely furnished apartment. He had sent his wife and children to stay with neighbours, to avoid any embarrassment or, God forbid, unintended offence. SS Officers were totally unpredictable; anything could happen.

The painting was hanging in its usual place above the sideboard. Krakowski had been painstakingly briefed by Mandel earlier that day. He had been told what to say and how to say it, how much to ask for the painting, and how to explain why he wanted to sell it. He had also been told that the buyer would ask for a receipt. Krakowski had pen and paper ready as instructed, and was waiting for his visitors to arrive.

Mandel opened the door and let the major and his guest enter. Ignoring Krakowski completely, the major walked over to the sideboard and pointed to the painting. 'This is it, Herr Fuchs,' he said. 'I hope this is what you are looking for.'

Krakowski watched the tall young man follow the major across to the painting. Impeccably dressed in a grey double-breasted suit, white shirt, silk tie and black shoes so shiny they almost sparkled, the young man pulled a silver cigarette case out of his pocket. Turning to the major, he offered him a cigarette and they both lit up.

'This is a truly remarkable painting,' said the young man. He bent down to look at the signature at the bottom of the painting. 'A Monet, no doubt about it. And you wish to sell it, Herr—?'

'Krakowski,' interjected Mandel.

'Krakowski,' repeated the young visitor. Krakowski then went through the prearranged charade and said all the things he had been instructed to say. After that, it only took a few minutes to complete the transaction. The major and his satisfied guest then swept out of the room, followed by the driver, carrying the painting under his arm.

Krakowski slowly closed the door, and then turned and stared at the empty space above the sideboard. He felt as if part of his life had been torn away from him, never to return.

For the next hour, Krakowski wandered aimlessly through the ghetto until he found himself in front of Herzl's studio.

'You look like you've seen a ghost,' said Herzl, looking at his friend. 'Come in.'

Herzl reached behind his bunk and pulled out a half-empty bottle of schnapps, a precious commodity obtained on the thriving black market. Krakowski took a swig, the schnapps burning the back of his throat with welcome pain. 'Cheer up. Not all is lost, my friend,' said Herzl. 'You still have this – remember?' He pointed to the painting on the easel. 'I framed it for you this morning.'

Feeling better, Krakowski walked over to the painting and looked at it. 'My God, David, I could swear it's the real thing. Thank you.'

Herzl smiled. 'Take it home, my friend,' he said. 'It will make you feel better. Also, for your family's sake …'

'You're right; I'll do that.'

Herzl took the painting off the easel and handed it to his friend.

'I can't tell you what this means to me,' said Krakowski. He reached into his pocket, took out two small gold bars and placed them on the easel. 'Take this, it's for you. This is what they gave me for the painting. I can't keep it. The painting was never for sale.'

'I understand,' said Herzl and gulped down the last of the schnapps in the bottle. 'We'll buy some more of this.'

What Krakowski couldn't have known was that the gold given to him in payment for the painting by the impeccably dressed young man, was dental gold. Gold that had been harvested from the bodies of dead Jews in the concentration camps. Gold fillings and bridgework mainly, broken out of the jaws of the corpses by other Jews, doing the unthinkable to stay alive. This gold was then melted down, and often mixed with gold from other sources – such as gold looted from other victims' possessions on their way to the gas chambers – to disguise its true origin. It was then stamped with the German eagle insignia, the *Reichsadler,* and given a new, 'respectable' identity acceptable to the Swiss bankers before being transferred to 'neutral' Switzerland, to finance the war.

What Krakowski didn't know either was that Herzl had exchanged the painting in the original frame with his copy, and that the painting a very dejected Krakowski was carrying home was in fact his original Monet, given to him by the famous artist himself on that sunny afternoon in the master's garden many years ago.

* * *

'Anyone for more coffee?' asked the countess.

'Yes, please,' said Tristan. 'Now that we've met Herzl, the master forger in Warsaw, how did he end up in Treblinka?'

'Kun told me. Over coffee and cake in Café Gerbeaud, his favourite establishment in Budapest. It's quite a story; you'll love it,' said Jack, enjoying the warm sun on his back.

'Another story? How surprising,' said the countess and stood up. 'I'll get some more coffee, but don't start without me.'

'I won't, promise.'

* * *

'It all began with the Warsaw Ghetto Uprising in April 1943,' said Jack. 'Arguably one of the most significant acts of Jewish resistance during the war. Herzl was part of the Jewish Combat Organization that began to build bunkers in the ghetto and smuggled weapons and explosives into the ghetto, which were later used during the uprising. The uprising was an act of Jewish resistance to oppose the transportation of the remaining ghetto population to the death camps, after more than a quarter of a million Jews had been transported to Treblinka and killed as part of *Grossaktion Warschau* in 1942.'

Jack poured himself another cup of coffee and looked pensively across the canal to the other side. For a moment he felt like he was looking across the Rubicon to a past of unimaginable mass murder and death on a scale that was difficult to comprehend.

'The Postmaster of Treblinka's story starts when Herzl was captured in one of the bunkers by the Germans towards the end of the uprising in May 1943,' continued Jack, 'and brought before the police commander SS-Brigadefuehrer Jürgen Stroop for interrogation.'

Warsaw Ghetto: 1 May 1943

SS-Brigadefuehrer Jürgen Stroop, a ruthless man without moral compass, was feeling pleased with himself. It had been a good day. Since taking charge of the suppression of the Warsaw Ghetto Uprising on 17 April, considerable progress had been made. The way he had dealt with the uprising was both simple and effective. He realised the only way to snuff out the embarrassing uprising was to burn down the entire ghetto, building by building, and blow up the larger structures like the Great Synagogue, which was of great symbolic significance to the resident Jews.

Stroop methodically prepared a daily report of his activities in the ghetto. As he documented on 1 May 1943, which would become part of his detailed report, *The Jewish Quarter of Warsaw is no more!*

He stated: *'Progress report of a large-scale operation on 1 May 1943: Start 0900 hours. 10 search parties were sent out, and a larger battle group was dispatched to clear out a certain block of buildings, with the added instruction to set fire to the buildings.'*

And then, further down in the report: *'In today's operation a total of 1,026 Jews were caught, of whom 245 were killed, either in battle or while resisting. In addition, a considerable number of resistance fighters and ringleaders were also caught.'*

One of these was David Herzl, a well-known ringleader of the uprising. Stroop had him brought to his car. He was curious. He couldn't understand how Jewish resistance fighters, whom he considered to be *Untermenschen*, could put up such a valiant fight against two battalions of Waffen-SS.

Stroop got out of his car, lit a cigarette and looked at the emaciated wretch standing between two burly Security Police officers in front of him.

'So, you are David Herzl. Master forger, explosives expert and resistance ringleader.'

Herzl didn't reply. Realising his death was imminent, he just looked at Stroop with contempt.

'You must have known from the beginning that there was no way the uprising could succeed. All you did was accelerate the death of thousands, and bring about the destruction of the ghetto. Look around you. So, I ask, what was the point of it all? Can you help me with that?'

Herzl took his time before replying. 'I'm not sure I can help you, but there was definitely a point to it all, which someone like you may not be able to see or understand.'

One of the police officers was about to hit Herzl with the butt of his rifle. To talk to Stroop like that was unthinkable, but Stroop held up his hand to stop the blow.

'And what may that be? Humour me.'

'It's called freedom to choose. I want to be able to choose the time and place of my death, not leave it to someone else to decide.'

'Hm. So, how good a forger are you?' asked Stroop, changing direction.

'The best,' answered Herzl, surprised by the unexpected question.

'All right. Let's put it to the test, shall we?'

'What do you mean?'

'I will let you choose the time and place of your death, but there are conditions.'

'What kind of conditions?'

'You will be given an original painting by one of the old masters. If you can make a copy that is true to the original so that a panel of experts cannot tell the copy from the original, I may let you live. If you fail ...' Stroop shrugged. 'You know the answer. So, as you can see, it's all up to you. Your death is in your hands. What do you say?'

Herzl looked at Stroop, unsure if he was joking. *They are all mad,* he thought. 'Will I be given all the materials I would need to meet such a challenge?' he asked. 'Without that, there's no point.'

'Of course.'

'In that case, I accept,' said Herzl.

'Excellent! I'll arrange it. Take him away!'

What Herzl couldn't have known was that there was calculated purpose behind the challenge. Stroop, an ambitious man and eager to please his superiors, knew that SS Captain Theodor van Eupen, the commander of the Treblinka labour camp, was always on the lookout for talented painters who could restore paintings, looted from the museums of occupied countries, passing through Treblinka on their way to Germany. Van Eupen considered himself something of an art connoisseur, who was equally as eager as Stroop to impress his superiors in Berlin, with regular deliveries of priceless looted art treasures that he had meticulously restored by Jewish artists working for him in the camp. If Herzl was as good as his reputation seemed to suggest, then he could be a valuable commodity Stroop could use to impress Van Eupen in Treblinka, which was only a hundred kilometres away.

* * *

'So, what happened?' asked the countess. 'Was there a challenge?'

'There sure was,' said Jack, enjoying himself. 'Herzl was given a painting by Jan van Eyck to copy. Stroop invited the commander of the Treblinka labour camp to be one of the judges, together with two other high-ranking SS officers in charge of processing Nazi plunder – or *Raubkunst* as it was known in the Third Reich.'

'And?'

'To cut a long story short, Herzl made a stunning copy of the painting that not only impressed the judges, but effectively saved his life. Instead of being executed as one of the ringleaders of the Warsaw Ghetto Uprising, Herzl was transferred to the Treblinka labour camp, given a "studio", all the materials he requested, and access to art galleries and curators in Germany to assist him in restoring some of the priceless art looted from museums in occupied countries, or confiscated from German Jews on their way to the gas chamber—'

'Did Kun tell you all this?' asked Tristan.

'Yes. Apparently, his mother, Ilona Kun, who was Herzl's assistant at Treblinka, lived to a ripe old age and told her son about all this. Stroop didn't walk away empty-handed either. He was commended for having spotted one of the most talented painters in the occupied territories, and for putting him to good use for the benefit of the Third

Reich. On 18 June 1943, Stoop was awarded an Iron Cross 1ˢᵗ class for having successfully put down the ghetto uprising, which had resulted in the killing of more than fifty thousand ghetto inmates and culminated in the destruction of the Great Synagogue on 16 May 1943. Stroop carefully documented all this in his detailed report, *The Jewish Quarter of Warsaw is no more!* Bound in black leather, it was presented in evidence during his trial after the war. The other copy Stroop had proudly sent to Himmler after the uprising had been crushed.

'What happened to Stroop; do you know?' asked the countess.

'He was convicted of crimes against humanity and executed in Warsaw in 1952. Ironic, don't you think?'

'Quite a story. So, Herzl is the man who became the Postmaster of Treblinka,' said Tristan. 'How did that come about?'

'I'll tell you,' said Jack, putting down his cup. 'You will remember I met Sandor Kun, Herzl's son, in Budapest last year in connection with the Bezukhova letter.'

'You mentioned this before, and it's all in *The Lost Symphony*, isn't it?' said the countess. 'The letter was central to the entire Russian story, right?'

'Yes. It was during that meeting I found out how Herzl became the Postmaster of Treblinka, and what that entailed. I can clearly remember my first meeting with Kun. It was an ice-cold morning. I was staying at the iconic Gellért Hotel in Budapest. This is what happened ...'

The chess game at the Gellért, Budapest: 27 February 2017

Just before eleven am, Jack walked down the imposing staircase of the Gellért Hotel, to meet Kun as arranged. Outside it was freezing and large chunks of ice were floating down the Danube, promising doom for anyone foolish enough to get in their way. He stopped briefly on each landing to admire the beautiful stained-glass windows depicting the ancient Hungarian legend of a magic stag, and prepared himself for what he knew would be a critically important meeting, perhaps even a watershed moment in his investigation.

The large foyer wasn't busy. The foul weather had kept most of the early morning regulars away. *That must be him,* thought Jack, and walked over to a well-dressed, elderly gentleman standing near the doors with a folding chessboard under his arm. 'Mr Kun?' said Jack, extending his hand.

'Yes. How did you know?' replied Kun in perfect English.

'The chessboard gave you away.'

'Ah. Have you been to the baths before, Mr Rogan?'

'No. I've only admired this grand establishment from the outside.'

'Then let me be your guide. You're in for a treat; come.'

Kun, a sprightly man in his seventies, moved with surprising agility for a man of his age. 'You know this is one of the biggest natural spring-water bath complexes in Europe,' he said, leading the way to the change rooms. 'It is famous for its spectacular Art Nouveau design. There are ten pools of various sizes and temperatures we can choose from. The place is a maze and usually very popular with locals like me. I used to come here twice a week and spend the whole day in here. Meeting friends and playing chess.'

'Budapest is very lucky to have something like this,' said Jack. 'I love the stained-glass windows and the beautiful tiles. And, of course, the old-world charm of the place.'

'May I suggest we have a swim first in one of the warm pools, followed by a sauna? Always a good start. After that, we can relax in the comfortable recliner chairs upstairs in the gallery, and have a game of chess. What do you say?'

'I'm in your hands.'

Kun was playing white. His opening move was e4. Jack responded with c5.

'Ah, the Sicilian Defence. Excellent move,' said Kun. 'So much has been written about this, especially by grandmasters like John Nunn and Jonathan Rowson. They attributed the popularity of this defence to its combative nature because it begins the fight for the centre of the board.'

'It does. A good friend of mine, a wonderful chess player who could play entire games from memory, told me to always open in this way. Apparently, a quarter of all games use the Sicilian.'

'Correct, and seventeen per cent of all games between grandmasters begin in that way.'

'And it is an excellent way to explore the strength of your opponent, especially if you are not familiar with his strategies and way of thinking,' said Jack, a sparkle in his eyes.

'Very good,' said Kun, obviously enjoying himself, and moved his knight to f3. 'Let's see if that's right.'

The game progressed quite rapidly after that, and Jack lost after putting up a valiant fight.

'I read your book about the Postmaster of Treblinka on the plane yesterday,' said Jack, introducing the subject that had brought them together.

'Konstantin told me about your intriguing encounter with David Herzl and his work,' said Kun, setting up the chessboard for the next game. 'What an amazing coincidence.'

'It must be the same man, surely, but I thought Herzl was killed in the Warsaw Ghetto Uprising in April 1943?'

'Not so. He was captured, and the Germans sent him to Treblinka. They needed him, you see. That's what saved him, and his ability to adapt.'

'Was it his talent for forgery?'

'In a way, yes. He was an outstanding painter, but he was also a pragmatist who found imaginative ways to survive. The Germans had looted artworks all over Europe – amazing stuff. In their usual, efficient way, they had set up a whole department dealing with this, and were restoring some of the more valuable masterpieces before sending them to Berlin.'

'Is that what Herzl was doing?'

'Yes. He actually had a studio in Treblinka and was working with art experts to restore paintings right up until the end of the war. He was exceptionally good at this, and that gave him privileges.'

'He *survived* Treblinka?'

'Yes. He was one of the very few who did, and so did his diary.'

'I understand that was the inspiration for your book?'

'Yes. It's an extraordinary record of what happened inside the death camp.'

'Where's the diary now?'

'In Prague. I gave it to the Jewish Museum. As a contemporaneous record it is invaluable.'

'I can see that. So, how did David Herzl, a master forger restoring stolen paintings for the Germans, imprisoned inside a notorious concentration camp, become the Postmaster of Treblinka, helping fellow inmates make contact with relatives and friends on the outside?'

'Ah. I knew you would ask that. As I mentioned before, Herzl was a pragmatist, a survivor. His unique situation in the camp gave him unique opportunities.'

'What kind of opportunities?'

'The most important – and most valuable – was contact with the outside world.'

'Seriously?'

'Yes. Concentration camps like Treblinka were strange places. Officials delivering and collecting paintings came and went all the time. They also provided him with the materials he needed to carry out his delicate, highly specialised work. A lot of it arrived by post, the *Feldpost*, a very efficient military organisation of the *Wehrmacht*, which became the general postal authority of the occupied territories like Poland. As part of his work, Herzl had access to this postal service and often wrote directly to suppliers, ordering materials, and corresponded with curators and other art experts with questions relating to his restoration work.'

'Fascinating,' said Jack. 'But how is this relevant?'

'You'll see in a moment. Another game?'

'Sure.'

A Rigó Jancsi at the Café Gerbeaud, Budapest: 28 February 2017

Jack was early. He arrived at the famous Café Gerbeaud on Vörösmarty tér just before ten am, sat down at a small marble table by the window, and ordered coffee. Established in 1870, this iconic establishment with its timeless, elegant interior had been the haunt of writers, politicians and artists for almost one hundred and fifty years, and had weathered two world wars, Russian occupation, and the bloody 1956 uprising. It was a haven of Hungarian social life that had welcomed such distinguished guests as the composer Franz Liszt, and Empress Elizabeth, Queen of Hungary, who was particularly fond of the wonderful ice-cream creations, which she pronounced 'the best ice in Pest'.

After several chess games at the Gellért – most of which Jack lost – Jack and Kun had agreed to continue their conversation the next day, as Kun had to leave early to catch the train back to his village. Jack had suggested they meet at the Gerbeaud, his favourite cafe in Budapest. This was eagerly embraced by Kun, who clearly enjoyed Jack's company and was already looking forward to another rare visit into town.

Inspired by Jack's enthusiasm and the intriguing content of the music box letter, Kun had promised to bring along some material he believed could be useful in assisting Jack in his quest.

'I'm sorry I'm late,' said Kun. 'Budapest trains.' He shrugged, took off his overcoat and sat down. 'No sweets?'

'I didn't want to start without you.'

'Ah, then let me remedy this at once.' Kun signalled to a waiter walking past and, speaking Hungarian, ordered two Rigó Jancsis.

'What's a Rigó Jancsi?' asked Jack. 'I understood that much. As for the Hungarian language, it's diabolically difficult.'

'It is,' conceded Kun. 'That's why it's always a good idea to take someone like me along. It's a Finno-Ugric language, like Finnish, Estonian and Lappic. Magyar is quite unique in Europe and, yes, very complicated. If you want to experience the real Budapest, you need a guide.'

'I'll keep that in mind,' said Jack, enjoying the banter.

'A Rigó Jancsi is a traditional Hungarian chocolate cake dating from the Austro–Hungarian Empire.' Kun smacked his lips. 'Delicious; you'll see. It's cube-shaped and has a touch of rum and vanilla in the filling. It also has quite a history.'

'Oh? Everything here in Budapest seems to have quite a history.'

'But this one is delightful. Let me tell you – the cake will taste so much better after you hear this: It's all about a Hungarian–Belgian love story.'

'How fascinating.'

'Rigó Jancsi was a famous gypsy violinist. Young, handsome, full of bravado and flair. He toured all over Europe with his own orchestra towards the end of the nineteenth century. One day, in 1896, he was playing in a restaurant in Paris and was asked to come to one of the tables to play a solo to show off his extraordinary skills. That's when he met Clara, the beautiful young wife of a Belgian duke. Enchanted by Jancsi's music and charm, she immediately fell in love and eloped with him, disguised as a gypsy. They lived together for ten years in various countries and squandered a fortune. She was the daughter of an American millionaire, which no doubt helped. During one of their visits to Budapest, Jancsi ordered a chocolate cake for Clara. She loved the cake, and the shrewd proprietor immediately named it after Jancsi. The Rigó Jancsi was born—'

'What a wonderful story,' interjected Jack.

'Unfortunately, this whirlwind romance didn't last. It came to an abrupt end when Clara met an Italian waiter and exchanged the violin for a bowl of pasta,' said Kun, laughing. 'Ah, here come our Rigó Janscis now. Let me know what you think.'

'Will do.'

'Speaking of remarkable love stories,' continued Kun, enjoying his Rigó Jancsi, 'I have another one for you that happens to be relevant to what we are about to discuss. I also have a surprise for you.'

'Oh?'

'It's about David Herzl.'

'The Postmaster of Treblinka?'

'Yes.'

'And the surprise?'

'Before we talk about that, I must tell you about the love story, because the two are connected.'

Jack reached for his notebook, opened it, and put it on the table next to the empty plate, which he had scraped clean right down to the very last morsel.

'I told you yesterday that Herzl survived the Warsaw Ghetto Uprising, was taken by the SS to Treblinka and put to work,' said Kun.

'Yes, restoring stolen paintings for the Germans.'

'Correct, but what I didn't tell you was that he had an assistant, a beautiful young Hungarian woman called Ilona. She too was a talented painter. They fell in love, and it was she who came up with the idea ...'

'What idea?'

'To introduce a little ray of sunshine and hope into the death camp.'

'How?'

'Because of his work, Herzl had free access to the Feldpost, the general postal authority established by the Wehrmacht in the occupied territories.'

'You told me.'

'It all began with a small, desperate request.'

'What kind of request?'

'One of Ilona's friends in the camp asked her if she could perhaps smuggle a letter out of the camp and send it through the Feldpost to her parents in Prague. She offered a valuable diamond ring as payment. When Ilona first mentioned this to Herzl, he dismissed the idea as absurd, but Ilona persisted. To cut a long story short, Herzl and Ilona managed to establish a sophisticated, underground postal network – involving people both inside and outside the camp – to facilitate the sending and receiving of letters through the Nazi Feldpost.'

'Seriously?'

'Yes. It even had a name. It was called the "Ballroom of Hope".'

'Strange name.'

'It is. They all knew they were dancing with death. If discovered, well, you can imagine ...'

'How macabre.'

'Hope often is.'

'You're right.'

'It was an ingenious set-up using contacts and bribes that went undetected right up to July 1944, when Soviet troops overran the camp. Despite risking their lives, Herzl and Ilona were among the few survivors.'

'Amazing.'

'But what is even more amazing is *this*,' said Kun. He opened his briefcase and put a bundle of papers on the table in front of Jack.

'What's this?'

'It's a copy of Herzl's diary. As I told you, the original is in the Jewish Museum in Prague. Another coffee?'

'Yes, please. I could certainly do with one. This is an incredible story.'

'Wait, it gets even better,' said Kun and began to sort through the pages in front of him. 'As part of his secret diary, which he must have kept carefully hidden, Herzl kept a meticulous record—'

'A record? Of what?' interjected Jack, sensing that something significant was about to be revealed. The butterflies in his stomach told him so.

'Herzl kept a record of all the letters he managed to smuggle out of the camp. Dates, names and addresses.'

'Why on earth would he have done that? Surely, if caught—'

'I was wondering about that too, but there's a simple explanation. This ingenious postal service was a two-way street. Not only did letters get out, there were quite a few replies as well, all addressed to Herzl. Using his records, he could then identify the intended recipient and pass on the replies. All part of a secret, underground postal service, right under the noses of the SS. The Ballroom of Hope. Brazen? Yes.

Desperate? Certainly. But surprisingly effective.'

'And this diary was like a dance card with death?'

'Sure, if the SS had found out about this ...'

'Unbelievable!'

'The bribes involved were huge, and this was what kept the wheels turning. Each letter cost a small fortune, but when you have nothing to lose ... a diamond on the way to the gas chamber is worthless.' Kun shook his head and looked sadly at Jack. 'Self-interest and greed in the middle of unimaginable slaughter, bringing a little hope, perhaps even joy, to the condemned.' Kun paused and looked at Jack. 'That was David Herzl's Ballroom of Hope.'

More breadcrumbs of destiny, thought Jack, shaking his head. He pointed to the bundle of papers on the table in front of Kun. 'How did you manage to get hold of this diary?' he asked quietly.

'It was left to me.'

'Oh? By whom?'

'Ilona Kun, my mother.'

* * *

'Wow!' said Tristan. 'That's quite a story, but the Bezukhova letter and your Russian adventure are now behind you. Anielka—'

The countess shot Tristan a stern look and shook her head. The wounds left behind by Anielka still ran deep, and emotional scars remained.

'You are right,' said Jack. 'In order to understand what Rabbi Stein told me, and why, you had to first enter the world of the Postmaster of Treblinka and his Ballroom of Hope. Without that, what I'm about to tell you would make no sense.'

'Is that why you went to Budapest to talk to Kun again?' asked Tristan.

'Yes.'

'And was it helpful?'

'It was.' Jack reached into his pocket, pulled out a sheet of paper and placed it carefully on the table in front of him. 'It's all about this.'

'What is it?' asked the countess.

'The last entry in Herzl's Treblinka diary. It records the postmaster's final letter he promised to deliver, but couldn't because by then it was too late. The line of communication had broken down. Treblinka II, the death camp, was being dismantled after the uprising in August 1943. The corpses were being dug up and burned, to erase evidence of the monstrous atrocities committed in the camp. The letter was the last, no, *the only*, collective voice of all the dead reaching out from the mass graves, trying to tell the world what happened. By then, the camp had been levelled and all evidence of its existence erased. A farmhouse for a watchman had been erected where the former bakery once stood, using bricks from the dismantled gas chambers, and the killing grounds had been ploughed over and lupins planted in an attempt to hide the evidence of mass murder. In a way, this letter, or more accurately what was attached to it, was all that remained at the time to tell the story of what really happened at Treblinka.'

'What do you mean?' asked the countess, looking a little confused.

'Apparently, attached to the letter was a detailed eyewitness account of what went on at the extermination camp between July 1942 and October 1943. This was the deadliest period of *Operation Reinhard*, the jewel in the obscene Nazi extermination crown: the Final Solution. For this reason alone, this record is invaluable. It was written by a man, a gypsy, who was forced to work in the *Sonderkommando*, which did all the unspeakable dirty work for the Germans like emptying the gas chambers and burying the corpses in mass graves. He therefore saw it all.'

'Do we know what happened to the letter?' asked the countess.

'Yes, and no,' replied Jack. 'That's the mystery here, and the challenge – *my* challenge.'

'The spectre of destiny again?' said the countess, raising an eyebrow.

Jack shrugged. 'Stein seems to think so.'

'Can you enlighten us?' said Tristan, who could see where this was heading.

'Sure. Herzl and Ilona were two of the few Treblinka survivors. Out of some nine hundred thousand victims who were murdered, only sixty-seven were still alive when the Russians liberated the camp in August 1944. Everybody else had been shot before the Germans pulled out. They only survived because of the help and protection of Pavel Ustinov, a Russian Trawniki guard—'

'The Golem of Treblinka you mentioned in *The Lost Symphony*?' interjected Tristan.

'Very good! That's him. He was the one who sent Empress Alexandra's letter to Countess Bezukhova in France through Herzl's underground *Feldpost* network.'

'This is unbelievable,' said the countess. 'It's all interconnected, as if it were meant to be.'

'Stein almost used the same words,' said Jack. 'It was the delivery of the Bezukhova letter and what that triggered years later that made Stein turn to me with this. He called it a "golem mission". I call it a challenge.'

'A golem mission? How strange,' said the countess. 'How come he called it that, do you think?'

'It's all related to Pavel Ustinov, the Golem of Treblinka, and how he, Ilona and Herzl met. You will remember I wrote about this in *The Lost Symphony*.'

'You did. It was very moving,' said Tristan. 'Without Ustinov meeting Herzl, Empress Alexandra's letter would never have found its way to Countess Bezukhova, and without that letter, Kazanskaya Bogomater, the holy icon, would not have found its way back to the Alexander Nevsky Cathedral, and *Mat' Rossiya*, Tchaikovsky's lost symphony, would not have been discovered and given to the Russian people.'

Tristan paused and looked at Jack. 'I can see Rabbi Stein's point. It took a golem to make all this possible. And how it all came about is obviously significant, and must have been the reason Stein turned to you now, right?'

Jack nodded.

'So, let's have a closer look at this Golem of Treblinka, shall we?' said Tristan. 'All of this will make more sense once we do that.'

'It will,' said Jack.

The Golem of Treblinka, German-occupied Poland: August 1943

David Herzl sat in a small room allocated to him as his 'studio' in one of the barracks in Treblinka I, used to house the 'Trawniki' men. The Trawniki were Soviet prisoners of war trained by the SS as auxiliary police guards, deployed to guard the forced-labour camps as part of the Final Solution.

Herzl was trying to catch the last of the fading afternoon light to help him restore the halo of a Madonna. He preferred to work during daylight, as it was almost impossible to get the colours right otherwise. The harsh light from the single light bulb dangling from the ceiling was not conducive to meticulous restoration work involving priceless masterpieces.

'What do you think?' said Herzl and stepped back from the canvas.

'Perfect,' replied Ilona, his assistant. 'Giotto would be pleased. You are a genius.'

Herzl took Ilona by the hand and drew her towards him. 'This is surreal,' he said. 'Here we are in this shabby little room in the middle of a concentration camp where hundreds are killed every day, surrounded by works of genius worth millions. Look over there, a Raphael, and there on my bed, a van Gogh and a Klimt. All looted from who knows where, and damaged along the way by ignorant thugs.'

'Patiently waiting here for a little restoration to return them to their former glory, by *you*.' Ilona gave Herzl a peck on the cheek. 'Just think how fortunate we are—'

'Useful, would be a better way to put it,' interrupted Herzl, well aware that it was only his talent that kept them both alive. He had even survived the Warsaw Ghetto revolt in May, only because of his reputation as a master forger. Instead of being shot with all the others, he had been spared and sent to Treblinka for 'special duties'. 'As long as we are useful, they'll keep us alive.'

'Hush,' said Ilona and placed a finger on Herzl's lips to silence him. 'Don't question fate, it's bad luck.'

'I know, yet here we are, getting preferential treatment and more food than we can eat. Yet out there, they are starving on their way to the slaughterhouse. It's obscene. I wish I could do something—'

'You *are*.'

'The letters?'

'Yes. They mean a lot more than a little extra food. A lot more than you realise. Hope is priceless, and communicating with those we love, precious.'

'You think so?'

'I know so. You should have seen Roza's face when I told her that her letter had been dispatched and was on its way to her mother in Prague.'

Herzl began to chuckle and said, 'Delivery with compliments of the Feldpost.' He got huge satisfaction out of the unique arrangement he had on the go right under the noses of the SS. He felt it gave him a little power and self-respect.

For several weeks now, he had been able to smuggle letters written by fellow prisoners out of the camp as part of his own correspondence to order materials, or consult art experts throughout the Reich in connection with his work. These letters were never questioned by those in charge, as the *'Restorierer'*, as Herzl was known, was under the personal protection of SS Captain Theodor van Eupen, the commandant of the Treblinka labour camp. Treblinka II, the horrific killing machine, was located a mile away in the forest, and had a different commandant who reported directly to Operation Reinhard.

Whatever Herzl asked for, Herzl got. His work was that important, and van Eupen, who considered himself something of an art connoisseur and frequently visited Herzl, used it to impress his superiors in Berlin. They welcomed the regular deliveries of priceless art treasures from Treblinka, meticulously restored by Herzl, and praised van Eupen accordingly.

Herzl and Ilona sat on Herzl's bed, holding hands. Outside it was already dark. They were listening to the Trawniki singing soulful Russian songs full of sadness and longing, when there was a knock on the door. Herzl got up, opened the door and looked at the mountain of a man standing outside.

'I hear you speak Russian,' said the man, his voice deep and melodious.

'I do. What is it you want?'

'I've come to warn you,' said the man, lowering his voice.

'Warn me? What about?'

'The letters ...'

'I ... I don't know what you mean,' stammered Herzl, suddenly feeling sick.

'May I come in?'

Herzl stepped aside and let the man enter.

'We are safe in here as long as they are singing outside,' said the man, recognising the fear in Herzl's restless eyes. In the camp, fear was never far away, and life could be snuffed out in an instant and for no apparent reason.

Ilona stood up and looked at the huge man, who almost filled the room with his presence. His curly beard and unkempt hair gave him a wild look, but his voice was seductively gentle, and seemed at odds with his powerful physique and threatening appearance. *He has kind eyes*, thought Ilona as she kept watching the man's body language.

Herzl pointed to the only chair in the room. 'Please sit.'

'There are whispers,' said the man, sitting down.

'What kind of whispers?' asked Herzl.

'That you are smuggling letters out of the camp.'

Herzl looked at Ilona and locked eyes with hers. She too understood Russian.

'Don't worry, you are safe – for now,' continued the man. 'Roza is a friend. I give her extra food when I can.'

So, that's her guardian angel, thought Ilona, who knew Roza well. *Her golem. He certainly looks like one.*

Used to dealing with the unexpected, Herzl realised there was no point in playing a charade of denial and instead decided to find out what had brought the man to him, alone, and at this hour. 'Why are you doing this?' he asked, taking a dangerous leap into the unknown.

'Why the warning?'

'Because I need your help, and I can help you in return. In short, we can help each other.' With that, the man began to relax.

'Please explain.'

'My name is Pavel Ustinov. I'm from Yekaterinburg. Do you know where that is?'

Herzl nodded.

'I was captured by the Germans during the battle for Moscow at the end of 1941 and have been a prisoner of war ever since. I was trained as a Trawniki guard by the SS in a camp outside Lubin last year. And now, here I am.'

'Why are you telling me all this?' asked Herzl.

'Because I need your help,' repeated the man.

'What kind of help?'

'You can help me fulfil a promise.'

Herzl looked at Ustinov, surprised. 'I don't understand. What kind of promise?'

'A promise I made a long time ago to someone who was kind to me when I was in need. I grew up in an orphanage inside a monastery in Yekaterinburg.'

'What kind of promise?'

'The nun who took me in when I was a starving little boy and looked after me, was dying just as the monastery was being closed down by the Bolsheviks in 1920. I was twelve. She handed me a letter and asked me to guard it with my life because it was very precious.'

Ustinov paused and ran his thick fingers through his unruly hair, painful memories clouding his craggy face. 'She also asked me to deliver it, whatever it may take, and I promised to do just that,' said Ustinov, his voice barely audible. 'Then, she died in peace,' he whispered.

'What kind of letter?'

'I don't know. It's in a sealed envelope with a name and address on it.'

'But that was twenty-three years ago,' interjected Ilona. 'You kept the letter all these years?'

'I did. There's no time limit on a promise. I had it on me all the time. On the battlefields, in the prison camps, in the field hospital, always. In fact, I have it with me right now.'

Ustinov reached into his shirt pocket and pulled out a crumpled envelope. 'This is it here.'

'May I see it?' said Herzl.

Ustinov handed him the letter.

'Hmm. It's addressed to a countess in France. How interesting.'

'I don't know if I will ever get out of here alive, and I can't stop thinking about that promise. It's keeping me awake at night. I'm afraid that time is running out.'

'You are taking a big risk coming to me with this,' said Herzl.

'Roza said I can trust you. And besides, aren't we all taking big risks here every day? I have nothing left to lose, except this letter here.'

'I understand.'

'Do you think you could smuggle it out of the camp and send it to the countess in France through the Feldpost?'

Herzl looked at Ilona. She nodded ever so slightly.

'I suppose I could.'

'I cannot pay you like the others. I know that substantial payments are needed to make all this work, both here inside the camp and outside.'

'You are well informed. You know how these things work in here. Yes, substantial bribes are needed to make this possible, but even then the risks are great. And there are no guarantees. Anything can happen to the letter along the way.'

'Trying is better than doing nothing. I am happy to take that risk. While I cannot pay you, I don't come empty-handed.'

'What do you mean?'

'I can offer you something more valuable than payment.'

'Oh? What?'

'Protection. I have influence among the guards and they look up to me. I can make sure your secret stays safe, a blind eye is turned when needed and no questions asked. The SS are lazy and leave the work to us. How does that sound?'

'Too good to be true. What do you think, Ilona?'

'I think with Pavel's help we could perhaps even expand our little operation, and you could become the Postmaster of Treblinka,' said Ilona, a sparkle in her eyes.

'Did you hear that, Pavel?'

'I did. I think Ilona's right. I am a prisoner in here just like you two, not expecting to live. If we can make a little difference in this hellhole and bring a little hope and sunshine into a few lives, like you did for Roza, then please count me in.'

'All right,' said Herzl and held out his hand. 'Leave the letter with me.'

'Thank you. I can't tell you what this means to me. You won't regret this,' said Ustinov, tears in his eyes. 'I better join the others outside, or they'll wonder where I am. The next song is my turn and besides, I play the balalaika.'

* * *

'Did this help?' asked Jack. 'Are we getting any closer to understanding Stein's motivation, and why he turned to me with this after all these years? Why now? *Why me?*'

'It's obvious, isn't it?' said Tristan. 'Because he realised you were possibly the only one who could pull this off, right? If you succeeded – against all odds it would seem – in locating and interpreting Alexandra's letter, then why not this one?'

'I suppose so,' said Jack, laughing. 'Just before the Liberation, Herzl took his diary and the letter entrusted into his care to Budapest, where Ilona's family lived. He was quite ill by then, and became obsessed with delivering the letter, just like Ustinov was obsessed with delivering Alexandra's. All Herzl had was a name and an address in Italy. Both are recorded in his diary, which survived. This is it here ...'

'And did he?' asked Tristan. 'Deliver the letter?'

'We are not sure. Ilona was pregnant by then, expecting her first child – Sandor – but Herzl insisted on making the journey to Italy to deliver the letter. He left Budapest in July 1945, and didn't return.'

'Do we know what happened to him?'

'No. You must understand that the whole of Europe was in chaos after the war. Travel was difficult and dangerous, if not impossible. And he was a sick man.'

'So, what *have* you got?' asked the countess.

'The name of the sender and a delivery address, kind of. The letter was sent by Anibal Santi, a gypsy, on behalf of his father, Django Santi, and was addressed to someone called Claudio Alberti, care of the village priest at Arquà Petrarca, a small township near Padua here in northern Italy. Not far from here, actually.'

'Is that it?' said Tristan, shaking his head.

'It is, but we've had much less to go by with other matters ...'

'True,' conceded Tristan.

'And I suppose you want to find out if Herzl made it to the village and did in fact deliver the letter?' said the countess.

'Yes.'

'And, if possible, find it, and the Treblinka records,' said Tristan.

'That's the idea. They would be invaluable. You can see that, can't you?'

'Sure. At least it isn't far; sixty or so kilometres. I visited there several times with Lorenza's mother,' said the countess. 'It's one of the most picturesque villages in Italy. You could be there in an hour.'

Jack looked at Tristan and smiled. 'Do you feel like a picnic, mate?'

'Why not? Looks like a lovely day.'

The countess sighed and stood up. 'I'll ask the kitchen to prepare something for you. At least you won't be doing your sleuthing on an empty stomach.'

'Would you like to come along?' asked Jack.

'No, thank you. This sounds like secret men's business to me.'

'You could be right there,' said Jack and slapped Tristan good naturedly on the back.

'Just don't get into trouble – again,' said the countess on her way to the door.

'You have Isis's number, don't you? Just in case,' teased Jack, and gathered up his papers. 'We can always rely on the Time Machine cavalry to bail us out, can't we?'

'Incorrigible rascals, both of you!'

'We can live with that, can't we, Tristan?'

Arquà Petrarca: 5 August 2019, morning

As the water taxi approached the Rialto Bridge on their way to Piazzale Roma, where the countess's car was parked, Tristan looked up at one of the palazzos, and a strange feeling of recognition he couldn't quite place washed over him. The palazzo looked empty and neglected, but the crest above the imposing entry facing the canal hinted at a glorious past, and an illustrious family that had once called it home.

What Tristan didn't know at the time was that the crest above the entrance was that of the Alberti family, and that he had just passed the palazzo where Isabella had given birth in secret to an illegitimate child in 1924. What Tristan didn't know either, was that he had just looked up at the birthplace of the author of the letter Jack was trying to find, and that he had once again witnessed destiny at work; all part of an extraordinary story about to unfold.

Tristan turned to Jack sitting next to him. 'What do we know about Arquà Petrarca?' he asked. 'I saw you looking it up just before we left.'

'Apart from the fact that it is one of the most picturesque villages in the Euganean Hills close to Padua, with beautiful stone buildings and a long history dating back to the Bronze Age, its claim to fame is the poet Petrarch.'

'How come?'

'The illustrious Renaissance poet spent the last years of his life in the village and is buried in the churchyard of Chiesa di Santa Maria Assunta, the main church of the village. The church will be our starting point because the letter was addressed to the village priest.'

'Makes sense.'

The trip from Venice to Arquà Petrarca took just under an hour. Traffic was light, and Jack enjoyed the power of the BMW as it climbed into the scenic hills, the fields of vines either side of them promising a rich grape harvest.

Jack pointed ahead. 'Almost there. What do you think?'

'Stunning place. Looks like time stood still here.'

46

'Let's hope so. It would make things a lot easier for us if it has.'

'I suspect that may be wishful thinking. On the outside, perhaps, but I don't know about inside.'

'Let's go and find out, shall we?' said Jack as he pulled up next to the church. 'A lot can happen in seventy-three years.'

Inside, the church was cool and silent. Apart from a woman dressed in black, preparing flowers at the altar, the church was empty. Jack walked up to the woman and pointed to the altar. 'This is stunning, and with statues on both sides,' he said.

'Mary and the angel Gabriel. We are very proud of it here. It's the work of Francesco Rizzi, and the altarpiece here is the work of Palma the Younger. We also have frescos dating from the eleventh century, Venetian–Byzantine school. Over there.'

'Impressive. Where can I find the local padre?' asked Jack.

The woman pointed to the entrance. 'He's just come in. That's him over there: Father Armantini.'

Jack walked up to the padre – an elderly man well in his seventies – and introduced himself. He decided to come straight to the point.

'I know this may take us back many years, Padre, but do the names Anibal or Django Santi, and Claudio Alberti mean anything around here?'

Tristan thought he could see surprise and a flash of alarm in the padre's eyes. It only lasted for an instant, but Tristan had noticed it. So had Jack.

'The Alberti family has had a long association with this village. They lived here for generations and had substantial landholdings. Claudio Alberti was the last one. I've been here for more than forty years, but he had left by the time I arrived. Sold everything and left the village.'

'I see. What about Anibal Santi?'

The padre shook his head. 'The name doesn't mean anything to me.'

'There's just one more,' said Jack. 'David Herzl; does that name—?'

'No!' said the padre, looking uncomfortable. 'Why do you ask?'

'It's a long story. There's no need to trouble you any further, thank you.'

'No trouble at all,' said the padre, looking relieved. 'Have a nice afternoon, gentlemen.' With that, he turned and hurried out of the church.

'We seem to have touched a raw nerve there; what do you think?' said Tristan.

'I agree, but—'

'There's more to all this,' said the woman at the altar. 'I couldn't help overhearing ...'

Jack spun around. 'Oh? *There is?*'

'Yes. A lot more. Every village has its secrets.'

'What kind of secrets?' asked Jack.

'You should talk to my daughter. She's a local historian and tour guide.'

'Where can we find her?'

'By Petrarch's tomb outside the church. She's just giving a Petrarch tour to some tourists.'

'Thank you,' said Jack. 'That's most helpful.'

Tristan pointed to the stone floor, rubbed smooth and shiny by the footsteps of generations past. 'Can you see it?' he said on their way out.

'What?'

'Breadcrumbs,' replied Tristan, smiling.

Jack could see a group of Japanese tourists standing in front of an imposing stone memorial – Petrarch's tomb. A tall, middle-aged woman was addressing them: 'Best known for his "Book of Songs", a collection of three hundred and sixty-six poems of unrequited love involving a married woman he called Laura, Petrarch, celebrated scholar, author and humanist, is considered one of the founders of the Renaissance.'

The woman watched Jack and Tristan walking towards her. 'Do you mind if we join the tour?' said Jack, giving her his best smile.

'You are welcome, please do.'

'In 2003, Petrarch's tomb was reopened,' continued the woman. 'That's when a disturbing discovery was made. The reason for reopening his tomb was to make a reconstruction of Petrarch's face from the shape of his skull, to mark the seven-hundredth anniversary of his birth. However, the DNA tests revealed that the skull in the coffin wasn't his ...'

'Not a good start,' whispered Tristan. 'I hope we can do better!'

The tour then continued to several other attractions in the village and concluded at Casa del Petrarca – Petrarch's house – which was now a museum.

Jack walked up to the woman after the tourists had dispersed.

'We met your mother in the church. She suggested we should talk to you,' he said.

'Oh? What about?'

'A mystery,' replied Jack, choosing his words carefully.

'What kind of mystery?'

'A mystery involving Claudio Alberti, Anibal Santi, and David Herzl,' said Jack softly. The look on the woman's face told him that he had chosen the right approach. She pointed to a house a little further down the hill. 'I live just over there. You better come with me. I'm Giana Sartori.'

'I am Jack Rogan, and this is Tristan Te Papatahi.'

'Interesting name. Where are you from, Mr Te Papatahi?'

'New Zealand.'

'Ah.'

'He can hear the whisper of angels and glimpse eternity,' said Jack, smiling.

'You don't say. I always wanted to meet someone who can do that; come.'

'May I offer you some tea?' said Sartori and pointed to a leather couch and chairs facing a stone fireplace.

'Yes, please,' said Jack and took a seat.

49

'Who is this?' called out someone from the back of the house.

Jack could hear the tapping of a walking stick coming closer. Then an old woman, well in her nineties, appeared in the doorway, her striking white hair pinned up in a bun.

'My grandmother,' said Sartori and walked over to the old lady. 'Come, sit with us, Nonna. I think you should hear this,' she said and took the old lady by the hand. Jack and Tristan stood up and introduced themselves. Her bent body might have been frail, but the old lady's mind was as sharp and lucid as that of a woman half her age.

'Mr Rogan and Mr Te Papatahi have come here to investigate a mystery.'

'Oh? A mystery you say? What about?'

Sartori turned towards Jack and held out her hand. 'Mr Rogan?' she said.

'We would like to find out if the names Claudio Alberti, Anibal Santi, and David Herzl mean something around here.'

'I haven't heard these names mentioned in a long time,' replied the old lady. 'Why do you want to know?'

Jack reached into his pocket, pulled out a piece of paper and put it on the table in front of the old lady. It was a copy of Herzl's diary entry recording the Django Santi letter he had promised to deliver.

Sartori stood up, walked over to a desk by the window and returned with a magnifying glass. Then she picked up the piece of paper and handed both to her grandmother.

'Can you tell me what this is all about, Mr Rogan?' said the old lady and put down the piece of paper and the magnifying glass, her parchment-like, almost translucent hands shaking.

Jack the storyteller didn't need much encouragement. First, he spoke about Treblinka, David Herzl and his Ballroom of Hope, and how a master forger became the Postmaster of Treblinka, bringing a little sunshine and hope into a place of unspeakable horror. Then he explained how the letters were dispatched by Herzl through the Nazi Feldpost under the very noses of the SS, and how a rabbi in Prague had thrown him a challenge and asked him to investigate the fate of the letter. Holding nothing back, Jack mentioned the eyewitness account that was apparently attached to the letter, recording the atrocities committed at the death camp before all evidence of its existence was erased by the retreating Nazis, eager to hide their deadly secrets from the world about to implode around them.

Sartori and her grandmother listened without interrupting, and then sat in silence after Jack had finished.

'That's quite a story, Mr Rogan,' said the old lady after a while, peering at Jack with sad, myopic eyes. 'I think I can help you fill in some of the gaps. Not all of them, but hopefully enough to show you the way. It all happened on a sunny afternoon in August 1945. A man walked into the village and asked to see the village priest ...'

Arquà Petrarca: 10 August 1945

Exhausted and frightfully thin, Herzl staggered into the village, his dirty, torn clothes, unkempt beard and long hair making him appear like a desperate vagabond best to be avoided. People in the village going about their business gave him a wide berth and quickly crossed the road to avoid contact. Herzl stopped at a fountain and began to drink greedily. Feeling a little better, he looked around.

It had been six weeks since he had left Budapest. His journey south through Austria had been arduous and slow, the devastation caused by the war and the Russian and Allied occupation that followed, taking their toll. Crossing into Italy through the rugged Tagliamento valley after leaving Innsbruck had been particularly difficult, as he had to rely on the charity of others, farmers mainly, to obtain a little food to stay alive.

He had walked most of the way, as hitching the occasional ride on a horse-drawn cart was a rare luxury. Public transport like trains or buses were virtually non-existent, and he had tried to stay out of townships and villages wherever possible to avoid being picked up without papers and questioned about his journey.

A woman walking past stopped and looked at the wretch leaning against the fountain.

'Are you looking for something?' she asked.

'Yes. The village priest.'

Surprised by the answer, the woman came closer, but the look in Herzl's feverish eyes made her stop. As a nurse, she had seen that look too often during the war, usually in the eyes of injured soldiers close to death.

'Father Angelis? You will find him in the church. It's just over there.'

'Thank you,' said Herzl and began to walk slowly towards the belltower he could see in the distance. Chiesa di Santa Maria Assunta, the main church in Arquà Petrarca, where the legendary poet had once worshipped, was an imposing building, especially for a secluded medieval village of modest size. The realisation that he had almost reached his destination made Herzl feel weak. Mustering the last of his remaining strength, he staggered up the few steps leading to the entrance, pushed open the door and looked inside. The spectacular altar beckoning in the distance looked like an ethereal beacon of hope, promising salvation. Herzl held up his hands in prayer and tried to walk towards it, but his tired legs wouldn't obey. Moments later, he lost consciousness and collapsed on the stone floor.

Father Angelis's housekeeper – Sartori's grandmother – was sweeping the floor near the altar when she heard a thump. She hurried to the open door to investigate. Unable to lift Herzl or even turn him over, she rushed into the sacristy to fetch Father Angelis.

It took two men to carry a barely conscious Herzl to the rectory. After some hearty food and some rest, Herzl was ready to talk.

'You were mumbling something about a letter when we brought you in here,' said Angelis, and pushed another bowl of vegetable soup towards Herzl, sitting at the kitchen table. The young housekeeper was standing at the stove, listening, and preparing the evening meal. 'Is that what brings you here?'

'It is. I was known as the Postmaster of Treblinka in the Nazi concentration camp near Warsaw—'

'*You were there?*' asked Angelis, surprised. He had heard some dreadful rumours about that camp and what had happened there.

'Yes. I was one of the very few who survived.'

'*You* were the postmaster?'

'Yes. It's a long story, a very sad one. And it is that story which brings me to your village. I have a letter with me I must deliver to Claudio Alberti. Does he live here?'

Angelis looked at Herzl, surprised. 'Yes, he does. He's a very prominent member of my congregation and a big landowner around here.'

Herzl looked at Angelis, the relief on his face palpable.

'Thank God! My journey is almost over then, and I will have kept my promise.'

'*Promise?* What kind of promise?'

'I made a promise to a desperate, condemned man to deliver a letter.'

Herzl reached into the pocket of his shabby coat, pulled out a flat, rusty tin and opened it. 'This is it here, addressed to Claudio Alberti.'

'Sent from Treblinka? Do you know who sent it?'

'Yes. A young man called Anibal Santi. He sent it on behalf of his father, Django Santi, who wrote the letter but was already dead by then. As was his entire family. Wife, children, everyone. Murdered. Sent to the gas chamber,' said Herzl with sadness in his voice. 'Like hundreds of thousands before them.'

Angelis looked at Herzl with shock and disbelief. 'Do you know what happened to the young man?' he asked, barely able to speak.

'He too was sent to the gas chamber. A few days after he gave me the letter and I promised to deliver it. Could you please take me to Alberti?' asked Herzl, wiping his face with the back of his hand.

'Do you know what's in the letter?'

'No. All I know it's the voice of many—'

'I'll take you to him; come.'

* * *

'So, you were there?' said Jack, surprised. 'But that was seventy-three years ago. He looked at Tristan sitting next to him, the fine hairs on the back of his neck beginning to tingle.

'I'm an old woman now, but I was young then, and had just started to work as a housekeeper for Padre Angelis when this happened,' said the old lady.

'And was Herzl taken to Alberti?'

'Yes, he was.'

'And he gave him the letter, I suppose?'

'He did.'

'Do you know what that was all about?'

'No, not as such, but Padre Angelis told me later that it shook

Alberti to the core. He was never the same after that. That's all I know.'

'Do you know what happened to Herzl?'

'He died a few days later; heart attack.'

'How sad,' said Jack.

'Yes, it was. We had no idea where he lived or where he came from; nothing. And he couldn't be buried in the cemetery here, either.'

'Why not?'

The old lady shook her head. 'He was Jewish. They buried him somewhere behind Alberti's house up on the hill.'

'After all that. A tragic end,' said Jack.

'But the Postmaster of Treblinka kept his word and delivered the letter,' said Tristan. 'That makes him an honourable man.'

'Yes, it does. That's what Padre Angelis told us at the time,' said the old lady. 'While he didn't officiate, he actually attended the funeral.'

'Is there anything else you can tell us about Alberti and the letter?' asked Jack.

'No, I can't. Nothing further was said about all this after Herzl died. But I don't think that was the end of it.'

'Why do you say that?'

'There were rumours, especially after Alberti passed away.'

'What kind of rumours?'

'Couldn't really say ...'

Or don't want to, thought Jack.

'But I know someone who could.'

'Who?' he asked.

'Father Armantini. He became the village priest here shortly after Padre Angelis was recalled to Rome and left. He was actually here when Alberti died. He and Angelis took care of everything.'

'What do you mean?'

'The scandal.'

'What kind of scandal?'

'You better talk to Padre Armantini about that,' said the old lady, looking quite distressed.

'I think we should leave it there, gentlemen, and let Nonna have some rest,' said Sartori and stood up. 'She gets a little confused when she's tired, especially when old memories are involved.'

'Understandable,' said Jack and stood up as well, gracefully accepting the dismissal.

'I will take you to Father Armantini if you like,' continued Sartori and headed for the door.

'We would appreciate that,' said Jack.

'As you can see, there's a lot more to all this,' said Sartori as they crossed the square in front of the church. 'Every village has its secrets, and secrets spread rumours. And rumours can be vicious and cause a lot of harm.'

'Are there such rumours concerning Alberti and the letter?'

'Yes. The rumours all have to do with his death. The way he died.' Sartori stopped and looked at Jack. 'You should look into that. It may give you the answers you are looking for,' she said, lowering her voice. 'Father Armantini could help you with that. He was there when it happened, and took care of everything.'

'Intriguing,' said Jack.

'It's more than that,' said Sartori. 'As you're about to find out. Here we are. You will find Father Armantini in the rectory. He's quite an unusual man. Charismatic for sure, but he can be a little fanatical at times. Plays by the rules – Church rules. Can be difficult. If he seems reluctant to talk about Alberti and his death, mention the Catechism released under Pope John Paul II, and refer to *grave sin*. That should do it. Clerics like Armantini are always afraid of the Church. Good day, gentlemen. It was nice to meet you.'

'Thank you. I'll keep all this in mind,' said Jack, trying to sort out the breadcrumbs that had been thrown at him in such an unexpected way.

'What do you make of this?' asked Tristan as they walked towards the rectory.

'Not sure, but she was certainly telling us something.'

'Telling us what?'

'Let's find out,' said Jack and knocked on the rectory door.

Venice: 5 August 2019, evening

By the time Jack and Tristan made it back to Venice, dinner in Osman's Kitchen, which was booked out as usual, was already in full swing. Countess Kuragin was in her element. Since taking over the running of the hotel and the restaurant after Lorenza's death the year before, the place had been thriving, and distinguished guests came from far and near to experience the unique cuisine of Osman's Kitchen, the famous Michelin Star restaurant, and enjoy the hospitality of Palazzo da Baggio, the luxury boutique hotel with its original antiques, paintings, and superb location on the Grand Canal near the Rialto Bridge.

Many of the guests were Kuragin regulars who had stayed at the Kuragin chateau outside Paris before the countess closed it after Anna, her daughter, had been found in outback Australia, and returned to France with her baby son. They still talked about the countess's famous soirees and marvellous dinner parties, and were hoping for more now that she was in charge of the splendid hotel in Venice everyone was talking about.

'Must have been quite a picnic,' said the countess as Jack and Tristan walked into the foyer.

'It was. In more ways than you can possibly imagine,' said Jack. 'Wait till you hear what we have to tell you.'

'Can't talk now. We are in the middle of dinner. Freshen up, and I'll send something to eat up to the terrace. I suppose you're starving, as usual. I'll join you as soon as I can. Must dash!'

It was well past eleven by the time the countess joined Jack and Tristan on the terrace above the restaurant.

'I could do with a drink,' she said and let herself fall into a chair. 'What a bumper night. All the regulars are back, and bringing their friends. We had a number of celebrities for dinner who are performing in the Teatro La Fenice.'

'You promised to take me, remember?' said Jack. 'You even gave me a choice: Rossini, Bellini, Donizetti or Verdi. I think I'll go for Verdi.'

'Soon, I promise. Leonardo is coming out of his shell. Deep down, he's a fabulous host, you know. Very popular with the guests.'

'Good to hear. Grief can be very toxic. What would you like?'

'Vodka martini, please.'

'Coming up,' said Jack, standing up.

'Ah. The famous notebook,' said the countess a few minutes later, sipping her martini Jack had prepared. She pointed to Jack's open notebook on the table. 'I can always tell you're onto something when I see you with that notebook.'

'Spot on,' said Tristan.

'A productive picnic, then?'

'You could say that, but it certainly wasn't a picnic,' said Jack. He closed his notebook and slipped the rubber band over it.

'Well, are you going to tell me?' asked the countess, leaning back in her chair.

Step by step, Jack recounted the events of the day, and told the countess how a chance meeting with a woman in the church led them to an old lady who remembered Herzl and the Treblinka letter, and what happened to him.

'Fascinating,' said the countess and held up her empty glass.

'Ah, but wait. The best is yet to come,' said Jack. 'I'll get you another one, and we'll tell you all about the crusty old Padre Armantini, and the secret rumours of Arquà Petrarca.'

'Can't wait,' said the countess, a sparkle in her eyes, and handed Jack her empty glass.

Arquà Petrarca: 5 August 2019, afternoon

If Father Armantini was in any way surprised or concerned to see Jack and Tristan at the door, he certainly didn't show it.

'Ah, I've been expecting you,' he said affably and stepped aside. 'Please come in.'

Jack looked at Tristan, raised an eyebrow and followed Armantini inside.

'You were? How come?'

'Because I now know who you are. Who *both* of you are. When we met briefly in the church earlier, I thought you looked familiar, but I couldn't quite place you. When I came back here, the penny dropped. You are Jack Rogan, the famous author who played a significant role in the Holy Father's recovery back in 2016: Lorenza da Baggio, the *Top Chef Europe* winner and the healing power of Ottoman cuisine? It was in all the papers.'

'You are right. And this is Tristan Te Papatahi, the late Lorenza's husband.'

'I am so sorry for your loss, Mr Te Papatahi. We couldn't quite believe it when we heard the tragic news of your wife's death last year.'

Tristan nodded, but didn't reply.

'And because of who you are, I concluded there must be more to your visit than a few casual questions about certain events that happened a long time ago, which few villagers would remember,' continued Armantini, watching Jack out of the corner of his eye. 'An author and high-profile adventurer like you, wouldn't just come here without a good reason.'

'You are right. There is a lot more to all this, Father. After we spoke to Signora Sartori and her grandmother, they suggested we come here and talk to you about David Herzl, and the letter he delivered to Alberti in 1945. Apparently, you know a great deal about the letter, Father Angelis, and Alberti's death, all of which are somehow connected. Is that correct?'

'I owe you an apology,' said Armantini, turning serious. 'When I told you back in the church that the names Anibal Santi and David Herzl didn't mean anything to me, I misled you. I hasten to add there was a good reason for this.'

'Please enlighten us, Father,' said Jack, trying to keep the sarcasm out of his voice. Having just witnessed Armantini admitting to being a liar, albeit in a subtle, roundabout way, Jack was curious to find out what he had to say for himself.

'As the village priest, I have a responsibility for the spiritual wellbeing of my congregation,' said Armantini, recovering quickly. 'The subject you have raised is very sensitive, even after all these years, and I saw it as my duty to protect the village from – how shall I put this? – painful probing into matters that have been put to rest a long time ago. Certain wounds may have healed, but can still bleed and cause a lot of pain.'

Jack looked at Armantini with renewed respect. The answer was ingenious, and could be taken as a sound explanation for what had transpired in the church.

'I completely understand your position,' said Jack, the tone of his voice conciliatory. He was trying to put Armantini at ease because he wanted his cooperation, not a confrontation that could easily end in an embarrassing communication breakdown. 'You can rest assured that everything you tell us will only be used with discretion, and in the most responsible way, as the last thing we want to do is open old wounds and make them bleed.'

Jack paused, collecting his thoughts. He was searching for the best way to reassure Armantini without misleading him or, worse still, scaring him away. 'Perhaps the best way to illustrate this is to tell you why we are so interested in this matter,' said Jack after a while.

Armantini nodded, obviously pleased with the answer.

'In coming here and asking these questions we had two objectives in mind: First, we wanted to find out if Herzl made it here after the war and delivered the letter. We had an address – this village – and a name: Alberti. In short, we wanted to find out if the Postmaster of Treblinka had been able to keep his promise. This question appears to have been answered in the affirmative, and leads me to the second, perhaps more important objective: Herzl's diary – which was left to his son, who lives in Budapest – refers to the letter and indicates that attached to it was an important eyewitness account of the atrocities committed at Treblinka, written by Django Santi, Anibal Santi's father. It is that priceless historical record – which may well be the only remaining reliable narrative of what happened to almost nine hundred thousand victims killed in the death camp – that we are interested in.'

Watching Armantini carefully, Jack paused to let this sink in. 'We want to find it. I'm sure you can see why,' added Jack quietly. 'It deserves to be preserved and take its rightful place for posterity.'

'I understand,' said Armantini, a troubled look on his face. He was obviously wrestling with something, but Jack's argument seemed convincing and difficult to brush aside. And besides, Jack was a well-connected man with friends in high places, and that included the Vatican.

'All right, I'll tell you what I know, but it may not be what you are hoping to hear. Then again, who knows where this may lead to and what doors it may open ...'

Smiling, Jack pulled his little notebook out of his pocket, opened it and looked expectantly at Armantini.

* * *

'What an exciting day you two have had,' said the countess, enjoying the cool breeze drifting across the canal from the sea. 'And did the padre give you something important that may open those doors? I've seen you do it often enough. Use a small piece of information to conquer the world. Your recent Russian adventure is a good example. It too began with a letter, and look where that ended up. I only hope this one will be a little less dangerous.'

'He certainly did,' said Jack, ignoring the comment, and pointed to Tristan. 'Why don't you take it from here? I'm interested in your interpretation of what Armantini told us. After all, you may have heard things I have missed. Not everyone can hear the whisper of angels ...'

'All right,' said Tristan. 'Let's go back to the beginning. Herzl walked into Arquà Petrarca in August 1945. He met Padre Angelis, the village priest at the time, and was taken to Alberti to deliver the Treblinka letter, which he did. A few days later, Herzl died and was buried somewhere behind Alberti's house. Nothing further is known about the letter, what it contained, or what happened to it. We must remember that Armantini didn't come to the village until much later, around 1965, when Alberti died – in controversial circumstances, it would appear. And that's when this story begins to get really interesting.'

'In what way?' asked the countess.

'Somehow, it all revolves around *how* Alberti died. At first, Armantini skirted around this subject. He clearly knew a lot more about it, but chose not to tell us until Jack stepped in and drew him out.'

'How did he do that?' asked the countess.

'I mentioned the Catechism released under Pope John Paul II in 1992, and referred to *grave sin*,' said Jack. 'Somehow, that did it. After that, Armantini opened up. It was Sartori who told me to do this. She obviously knows a lot about Armantini and how his mind works.'

'How weird. What was that about, and how was this relevant?'

'The *Catechism of the Catholic Church* is a very important document that outlines all the fundamental beliefs of the Church. It defines suicide as a "grave sin". As soon as I mentioned the Catechism, Armantini must have assumed that I knew, or at least suspected how Alberti died, and he stopped pretending. It all went from there.'

'Fascinating.'

'The circumstances of Alberti's death are the key here, because that's when the Treblinka letter surfaces again and plays a significant part in the story,' said Jack and opened his notebook. 'This is what Armantini had to say about that …'

Palazzo Alberti, Venice: 22 June 1965

Father Angelis knocked on Father Armantini's bedroom door. It was five in the morning and still dark.

'Come in,' said Armantini and sat up in bed. 'Something wrong?'

'I just had a phone call from Palazzo Alberti in Venice. Alberti's dead. His valet found him in his room …'

'Oh dear! What happened?'

'Don't know, but the valet sounded very upset. He said something horrible has happened and asked me to come as soon as possible.'

'Did he say what it was?'

'No. He could barely speak. I told him not to do anything or speak to anyone until we got there. We should leave straight away.'

'Absolutely. I'll get ready.'

Angelis and Armantini arrived at Palazzo Alberti on the Grand Canal near the Rialto Bridge two hours later.

An ashen-faced Mario Bonato, the elderly caretaker-cum-valet, who like his father before him had worked for the Alberti family all his life, opened the door.

'Thank God you're here,' he said. 'Come quickly, Padre!'

'Where is he?' asked Angelis as they followed Bonato to the stairs leading to the first floor.

'In his bedroom.'

'You did as I asked?'

'Yes.'

'Who else is in the house?'

'Only the cook and a maid. They live here, as you know. The others haven't arrived as yet.'

Alberti's bedroom was on the first floor facing the canal. Bonato opened the door and stepped aside to let Angelis and Armantini enter.

Angelis walked into the large, dimly lit room, and gasped. 'Is that how you found him?'

'Yes. I didn't touch anything. Just as you asked.'

'Good. Please leave us and make sure no-one enters the house,

64

clear?'

'Yes,' said Bonato and withdrew.

For a while Angelis and Armantini stood in silence, taking in the extraordinary scene in front of them.

The fire in the large marble fireplace had almost gone out. Only embers remained, looking like eyes of demons watching. The heavy curtains were drawn. The double bed by the tall windows facing the canal hadn't been slept in, the neatly arranged pillows and downturned blankets left just as the maid had prepared them the night before.

'I cannot believe what I see,' said Angelis, his hands folded in prayer as he looked at Alberti's body. 'What do you think happened here?'

'He hanged himself. Expertly, I'd say. Well planned. Formally dressed in a dark suit, white shirt and tie. Look at the rope around his neck and the chair, obviously kicked away ...' said Armantini. 'Poor man. What could make someone so desperate? Someone who had everything.'

'We can never look into someone's soul,' said Angelis. 'And I was his confessor for more than forty years ...'

Angelis walked over to the antique prayer chair at the foot of the bed. Something had caught his eye. 'Look at this,' he said and picked up a piece of paper left on the chair.

'What is it?'

'A suicide note, I'd say.' Angelis handed the piece of paper to Armantini.

All it said was: *I'm so sorry, my darling.*

'Do you know what this could mean?'

'I believe I do.'

'Can you tell me?'

'Later. What's this?' said Angelis and pointed to a small rusty tin on the chair. As recognition dawned, he picked up the tin and opened it, surprise and disbelief clouding his face. 'My goodness, I haven't seen this in years. I had no idea he kept it.'

'What is it?'

'Desperate voices from the past. It's all beginning to make sense.'

'You speak in riddles,' said Armantini.

'I will explain later. We have work to do!'

'What do you mean?'

'We have to avoid a catastrophe that could harm generations, and one man in particular.'

'I don't understand,' said Armantini.

'We can't just leave him like this. We have to cut him down and put him in bed. Alberti died in bed last night, understood?'

Angelis turned around and looked up at his friend hanging from the rafters with his face contorted in death. *'Not like this!* Come, help me.'

* * *

'No doubt about you two,' said the countess, rolling her eyes. 'The stories sure know how to find you. What else did Armantini tell you? Did it work?'

'Covering up the suicide, you mean?' said Jack.

The countess nodded.

'Yes and no would be the right answer here, I suppose,' said Jack. 'The family doctor came and found Alberti lying peacefully on his bed, fully clothed, I might add. No trace of the hanging remained, except visible marks around his throat. All other evidence had been removed by the two priests, and the staff in the building sworn to secrecy and silence. You must remember that Alberti and Angelis were powerful men, who between them ran the village and a lot more. Needless to say, the doctor did as he was told: he certified that Alberti died of a heart attack. I suppose in the end we all do, only the cause of it differs. Alberti was in his high seventies by then, so no-one would have questioned it.'

'One thing I don't understand here,' said the countess. 'Why did Armantini tell you all this when it appears to have been covered up at the time? Why tell you at all?'

'Ah, that troubled me as well, but the explanation is quite simple, really.'

'Oh? Tell me.'

'Let's not forget this is Italy.'

'What do you mean?' asked the countess.

'Venetians gossip. Everyone does. It's a national pastime. There was no way to keep this a secret, or cover it up completely. Word of a possible suicide got out almost immediately. Angelis did his best to keep the rumours contained, but they never went away. Not to this very day. In fact, they only got stronger, with more speculation about Alberti's death and why he killed himself.'

'Could the suicide note help here?' asked the countess. "'*I'm so sorry, my darling*"? Guilt? Remorse? *Darling?* What darling?'

'I asked Armantini about that. He said Angelis never spoke about it, but he suspected that he knew exactly what it meant.'

'What happened to the suicide note?'

'Angelis took it with him. It disappeared.'

'And what about that tin and its contents?'

'As you would have guessed by now, the tin contained Django Santi's Treblinka letter and the Treblinka records delivered by Herzl, the Postmaster of Treblinka, forty years earlier.'

'Do you think the suicide note and the Treblinka letter are linked?'

'I'm sure of it,' said Tristan. 'I could hear voices as soon as he mentioned the letter,' he added softly.

Jack shot the countess a meaningful look and shook his head.

'I suppose the crucial questions for you two are these,' she said: 'What happened to the letter? Does it still exist and if so, where is it? And most important of all, what was the connection between Anibal Santi and Alberti? Why did Santi send that letter to Alberti from Treblinka in the first place, and why was it so important to leave it behind with the suicide note? A desperate man's final act before falling into the abyss of death? A mystery for sure.'

'Correct,' said Tristan. 'Armantini told us that Angelis took the tin and its contents with him as well. Obviously, he wasn't going to leave something like this behind. He was recalled to Rome shortly after that. Armantini became the village priest and never saw Angelis again. Apparently, Angelis died in Rome a few years later. He was almost eighty by then.'

'So, where to from here, gentlemen? Is this the end of the Treblinka road?' asked the countess.

'Far from it,' replied Jack. 'In many ways this is just the beginning; isn't that right, Tristan?'

'I agree. I believe the letter still exists, just waiting somewhere to be discovered.'

'What makes you say that?' said the countess.

'I can *feel* it. It's calling out, because it's destined to take its rightful place and tell the world what happened,' said Tristan with sadness in his voice. 'So many dead. So much cruelty and violence. So much pain. The angels are weeping ...'

The countess stood up, walked over to Tristan and put her arms around him. 'Hush ... you can't carry all this alone.'

'He won't. We will share the burden, but first we must find the letter and the Treblinka records.'

'And how are you planning to do that?' asked the countess.

'By following those breadcrumbs you always talk about, and taking the next step.'

'And what might that be?'

'Palazzo Alberti is for sale. Has been for years. I made contact with an estate agent this afternoon and made an appointment. I have arranged an inspection for tomorrow morning.'

The countess shook her head. 'And what are you expecting to find?'

'Not sure. But we definitely want to talk to the caretaker.'

'Oh? Why?'

'Because he's the son of the valet who found Alberti hanging from the rafters. Who knows, he could throw some light on the reason Alberti killed himself. For once, gossip could come in handy; what do you think? They say behind every piece of gossip stands a kernel of truth. We just have to find it.'

'Did Armantini tell you that?'

'Yes, he did. It was his suggestion. I'm sure he had his reasons. Interesting gossip never dies, it just finds new places to hide.'

'And you are determined to find where that is?' said the countess, kissing Tristan on the cheek.

'You bet!' said Jack. 'Nightcap anyone?'

Palazzo Alberti, Venice: 7 August 2019

Jack and Tristan decided to walk the short distance to the palazzo near the Rialto Bridge rather than arrive by water taxi. This gave them an opportunity to discuss how best to approach the inspection, and how to involve the caretaker and bring up the subject of interest.

The agent, who had come all the way from Padua, was already waiting at the entrance, file in hand, and greeted them effusively. Interest in the palazzo, which was in poor condition and had been languishing on the agent's books for years, was almost non-existent. The rising water levels had scared away the few potential buyers, as the astronomical repair costs put the decaying structure beyond the reach of most. The agent was therefore most curious to find out who the interested party was who had contacted him out of the blue and asked for an urgent inspection.

After introductions, the eager agent launched straight into extolling the many attributes of the building, all of which were historical and referred only to the superb location, but ignored its present condition altogether. Jack looked at Tristan, shrugged, and let the agent prattle on until he realised that his clients were obviously not listening to what he had to say.

The agent stopped in front of the staircase and looked at Jack. 'May I ask what your interest is in this building?'

Jack had been expecting a question like that and was ready.

'Allow me to explain. Mr Te Papatahi here is the husband of the late Lorenza da Baggio, who sadly passed away last year. He is presently running the renowned restaurant Osman's Kitchen and the Palazzo da Baggio boutique hotel not far from here. I'm just a friend.'

'Ah!' said the agent, a glint in his eye. He realised at once that this was a serious enquiry with sales potential. 'I understand. Perhaps an extension to the hotel?' he probed.

'Perhaps,' said Jack. 'But before we can go any further, we need to clear up a few important matters, and they have nothing to do with the condition of the building as such, or its splendid location.'

The agent looked at Jack, surprised. 'Oh? What kind of matters?'

Jack turned to Tristan. 'Please, would you?'

'You may not be aware of this, but this building has a certain reputation around here,' said Tristan, watching the agent carefully.

'What kind of reputation?'

'The locals say it's haunted. Apparently, in 1965 Signor Alberti, who lived here for years, died in one of the bedrooms on the first floor in, let's say, suspicious circumstances. And there are certain other events prior to that which add to these rumours we would like to explore as well.'

The agent looked stunned. He was aware of the rumours, but hadn't expected his clients to know about them.

Tristan looked at Jack and winked. 'I'm sure you can understand our concerns,' he continued. 'If this were to be converted into, say, a hotel, for example, such a reputation could be fatal. Nobody wants to stay in a haunted hotel where somebody killed himself, certainly not the clientele we are used to.'

'I ... I understand,' stammered the agent. 'How do you suggest we address these issues?'

'We were told that a caretaker – a Signor Bonato – lives here, whose family has had a long association with the Albertis and this building. This may be helpful in clearing up the matter. If we could perhaps talk to him that would be a good start.'

'Sure. He lives at the back. I'll get him. Please give me a moment.'

'So far so good,' said Jack, smiling, after the agent had left. 'Estate agents are so predictable.'

'Greed always is,' said Tristan.

'I'm sure he'll brief the caretaker about all this, read him the riot act and make sure he cooperates. After all, a sale may depend on it. We'll have the caretaker's undivided attention, you'll see.'

'But will we have his cooperation? That's the question,' said Tristan.

'You may be right. Let's see; here he comes now.'

Alberto Bonato wasn't the kind of man Jack and Tristan had expected. In his late sixties, well-dressed, polite and softly spoken, he appeared more like a retired schoolteacher than a resident caretaker in a derelict building, waiting in vain to be sold. He walked confidently into the room and, ignoring the agent trailing behind him, introduced himself.

There's more to this man than meets the eye, thought Jack and shook hands with Bonato.

'I am so sorry for your loss, Mr Te Papatahi,' said Bonato, turning to Tristan. 'I attended your late wife's funeral last year. It was – if you allow me to say so – a spectacular event that clearly showed the high esteem and affection felt for her here in Venice.'

'Thank you. Very kind of you to say so,' said Tristan, a little taken aback.

'And to see Cardinal Borromeo officiate,' continued Bonato, undeterred, 'and read out a personal message from the Holy Father himself; well, that was a great honour indeed.'

'It was that. It was of great comfort to me, and the whole family felt very honoured.'

'And you, Mr Rogan, have a very special association with His Holiness, as I recall,' said Bonato, looking at Jack. 'You and the late Lorenza da Baggio were instrumental in bringing about the pope's almost miraculous recovery in 2016. The whole of Venice was talking about it.'

'Yes, yes, of course,' said the agent, butting in and sounding impatient. 'Mr Rogan and Mr Te Papatahi have some questions about the history of this building. So, if you don't mind—'

Bonato held up his hand. It was clear who was in control. 'Perhaps if I were to show you through the building first and tell you a few things about it, we could address your questions in a more meaningful way a little later?'

'Excellent idea,' said Jack, smiling. 'Lead on.'

'As you may know, this palazzo has been in the Alberti family since the sixteenth century,' said Bonato, beginning the tour in the formal rooms on the ground floor. 'Many a splendid function was held here in the ballroom, with dignitaries from all walks of life. The Church, the arts, writers, politicians, you name it. Especially after the war. Signor Alberti spent a lot of time here before making the palazzo his permanent home. That was in the late fifties. Before that, the family came here during the summer.'

Bonato stopped and pointed to a large chandelier. 'One of the few leftovers from that era; Murano glass. This room was, of course, lit entirely by candles before electricity was installed in the nineteen twenties. The dining room is over here. There was a wonderful flame mahogany dining table in here, seating twenty-four guests. Unfortunately, all the furniture was sold after Alberti's daughter died. Everything was removed. This place is now merely a shell of its former self. That was in 1988. She inherited the palazzo after her father passed away. She was the only heir.'

'I understand your family has been in service here for generations,' said Jack.

'That's correct. I grew up in this place. I have wonderful memories of that time, especially of Signor Alberti.'

'Oh? How come? You must have been quite young,' said Jack.

'I was about ten when Signor Alberti began to live here permanently. My mother was the cook, and my father a kind of valet-cum-caretaker. We all lived here under one roof.'

Jack nodded.

'Signor Alberti took me under his wing, you see. I know this sounds strange, but in a way we became friends. It was wonderful. It all started when I began taking breakfast up to his room on the first floor. Coffee with two boiled eggs, and toast. Always the same breakfast at seven am sharp. And it all went from there.'

'So, you knew him quite well?' said Jack.

'Oh, yes. He taught me to play chess. Then came the books. He introduced me to the joy of learning and took charge of my education.'

Bonato pointed to a large room at the end of a wide hallway. 'The library was just over there – thousands of books. Sadly, all gone now. He spent most mornings in the library and then went for long walks. He loved Venice.'

'His death must have come as quite a shock, I suppose.'

'It did.'

'Especially the way he died ...' said Tristan, watching Bonato carefully.

'You obviously heard the rumours.'

'We spoke to Padre Armantini yesterday. He told us. Your father found the body early in the morning, and Padre Angelis and Padre Armantini arrived soon after; isn't that right? And took control, so to speak.'

Bonato looked at Jack, surprised. 'You are very well informed.' He wondered why, thinking there must be more to all this.

'Could we see the room where it happened?' asked Tristan.

'Sure. It's upstairs. Follow me.'

As soon as Tristan entered the empty room on the first floor overlooking the canal and the Rialto Bridge, a strange feeling washed over him. Then he could hear voices, and sense anguish and pain, sorrow and remorse. And death. Tristan stopped in the middle of the room and looked up at the rafters. 'Here,' he said. 'It happened here.'

How can he possibly know that? Bonato asked himself, feeling suddenly quite cold.

'What happened?' asked the agent, sounding annoyed.

'Nothing,' said Jack. 'It doesn't matter. So, Signor Alberti's daughter inherited the palazzo after her father died; is that right?' he continued, changing the subject.

'Yes, she visited often, especially after her son became the Patriarch of Venice.'

'*The Patriarch of Venice*? What was his name?' asked Jack, barely able to speak.

'Contarini.'

Oh my God! It can't be, thought Jack as the small hairs on the back of his neck began to tingle. It was a familiar sensation.

'So, she was the mother of Marco Contarini, who later became Cardinal Contarini?'

'Yes, he came here often to see his mother. They were very close. A delightful man, very charismatic. He loved this place.'

Tristan was watching Jack carefully. He could see from the expression on Jack's face and his body language that he was wrestling with something profound.

'Isabella Contarini and her husband are buried in the Cimitero di San Michele. That's right, isn't it?'

'Yes, in the family crypt. How did you know?'

Jack could feel destiny at work, and took a deep breath to calm himself.

'It's a long story, he said, brushing the question aside. 'Would you mind joining us for dinner at the hotel this evening, Signor Bonato? I would very much like to continue this conversation with you then.'

'With pleasure,' said Bonato, surprised.

Looking quite pale, Jack turned to Tristan standing next to him. 'I think we have seen everything we need to for now, don't you think?'

'Absolutely,' said Tristan and followed Jack to the door.

'How did it go? Are you going to buy the palazzo?' teased the countess, a glint in her eyes as soon as Tristan and Jack walked through the door.

'Who knows?' said Tristan. 'But Jack seems to have had some kind of epiphany.'

'During a property inspection? How interesting.' The countess turned to Jack. 'Are you going to tell us about that?'

'Not yet. I have to do a bit more digging before we can call it a revelation. I've invited Signor Bonato to dinner tonight. I hope you don't mind.'

'Of course not, but who is Signor Bonato?'

'The caretaker at the palazzo,' said Tristan.

'He's a lot more than that, as you will see. I would appreciate it if you could join us for dinner,' said Jack.

'Sure, if that's what you would like. I'll arrange it,' said the countess. 'Perhaps in our private dining room, or on the terrace if the weather's good. Better than the restaurant. Privacy assured that way.'

'Excellent, thank you. All I can tell you is this: if I'm right, both of you are in for a big surprise. Bigger than you can imagine.'

The countess looked at Tristan. 'What do you think?'

'He could be right. What I felt in that bedroom where Alberti died was extraordinary. I think what happened in that room is the key here.'

Tristan looked at Jack. 'It's all about Isabella Contarini, isn't it?'

'Very perceptive of you, as usual,' said Jack. 'I believe it is.'

'No doubt about you two,' said the countess, rolling her eyes. 'Never a dull moment, that's for sure.'

Dinner at Palazzo da Baggio, Venice: 7 August 2019

Bonato arrived at seven pm sharp. Jack greeted him at the entrance and escorted him into the salon on the first floor.

'How magnificent,' said Bonato, letting his eyes roam and take in the historical splendour all around him. 'This is what Palazzo Alberti looked like before, sadly, it was dismantled. You are very fortunate to have all the original paintings and furnishings still here where they belong.'

'The same family still owns this place. That's the difference, I suppose.'

'In a way, the same family still owns Palazzo Alberti as well,' said Bonato. 'But times have certainly changed, and so have the circumstances – dramatically.'

'Please take a seat. Drink?' said Jack, digesting the surprising answer and its implications.

'Yes, please.'

'Before Tristan and Countess Kuragin join us—'

'Countess Kuragin?' interjected Bonato.

'The countess is a family friend who stepped in to help run this establishment after Lorenza's death,' Jack said. 'I would like to explain why we are so interested in Signor Alberti's death, and what happened at the Palazzo Alberti all those years ago. As you will see in a moment, it's quite a story.'

'I was hoping you would,' said Bonato. He sat down and looked up at the family portraits peering sternly down on him from above, each a da Baggio ancestor about to witness another of Jack's unique encounters with destiny.

By the time Tristan and the countess joined them and dinner was served, Jack had provided Bonato with a detailed account of the Postmaster of Treblinka's extraordinary story. Holding nothing back, he showed him the Herzl diary entry with the record of names and the Arquà Petrarca delivery destination that had started it all, explained the importance of the Treblinka eyewitness account, and emphasised why it was so important to find it and preserve it for posterity. Jack also alluded to Tristan's unique powers and reminded Bonato that the pope had personally married Tristan and Lorenza in the Sistine Chapel, in a gesture of gratitude for what they had done to save his life.

Jack and Tristan had decided that this frank and open approach would be the best way to ensure Bonato's cooperation and get access to crucial information he may be able to provide that could fill in the gaps in the story so far.

The countess, an experienced host, knew how to put Bonato at ease and make him feel welcome. The excellent dinner and wine helped as well.

'So, the Albertis and the da Baggios did business together in the past, you say,' she said.

'Yes, indeed. In a way they were rivals, competitors, but they were both merchants who made their fortunes trading with the Ottomans. Their family histories overlap, but there's never been intermarriage. Signor Alberti often spoke about that.'

'How fascinating.' The countess pointed to a portrait hanging above the sideboard. 'That's Osman da Baggio,' she said. 'Has Signor Alberti told you about him?'

'He sure has. Osman is the most famous member of the da Baggio family. And, of course, his recipes are legendary, especially since one of them recently saved the pope's life.'

'Hunkar Begendi,' said Jack. 'We just had it for dinner. Strange, how past lives overlap and are somehow intertwined, don't you think, Signor Bonato? His Holiness features again, doesn't he? In the Postmaster of Treblinka's story, I mean. Tristan certainly seems to think so, don't you, Tristan?'

'I do.'

'What makes you say that?' asked Bonato.

'I heard the whisper of voices in the room where Signor Alberti died,' said Tristan.

'And can you tell us what they were whispering about?'

'Not exactly. We were hoping you could perhaps help us here—'

'Padre Armantini told us what he and Padre Angelis found when they arrived at the palazzo on that fateful day Alberti died,' said Jack. 'But I'm sure you know all that. After all, it was your father who found Alberti and called Padre Angelis; that's right, isn't it?'

Bonato nodded.

Encouraged by Bonato's answers and demeanour, Jack decided to go a little further.

'Behind every rumour is a kernel of truth, correct?' he said quietly.

'You are right. There is.'

'Padre Angelis desperately tried to protect the Alberti name and reputation, didn't he?' continued Jack. 'That's why he covered up Alberti's suicide.'

'Yes. He and Alberti were very close. They had been friends for more than forty years.' Collecting his thoughts, Bonato reached for his glass and took a sip of wine. He knew exactly why he had been invited and what was expected of him. What wasn't quite as clear at that moment was how far he could go without compromising his loyalty to the Alberti family.

'But there was another, more important reason why Angelis wanted to protect the Alberti name, wasn't there?' probed Jack, watching Bonato carefully. He knew he was speculating here, which was always risky, but decided to press on regardless.

'Yes, there was.'

'And it all had to do with the Patriarch of Venice at the time?'

'Yes, he was Padre Angelis's protégé. Angelis had been mentoring him since childhood. He was destined for great things from the very beginning.'

'The Patriarch of Venice?' asked the countess. 'I don't understand.'

'Ah,' said Jack, smiling. 'My epiphany, as Tristan calls it. Amazing what you can find on the internet these days.'

'Could you please enlighten us,' said the countess, looking perplexed.

Enjoying himself, Jack sat back in his chair.

'Alberti had one child: a daughter, Isabella. His wife died in childbirth and he didn't remarry. Isabella married into another prominent family in the Veneto region, the Contarinis. It was an arranged marriage. She had a son, Marco, who, as Signor Bonato just told us, was destined for great things from the very beginning. He was already the Patriarch of Venice when his grandfather committed suicide, which according to Pope John Paul II's Catechism is a *grave sin*. This would certainly not have helped the career of Padre Angelis's protégé. How am I doing so far, Signor Bonato?'

'Surprisingly well, Mr Rogan.'

'I still don't understand,' said the countess.

'You will in a moment. Bear with me,' said Jack. 'The Patriarch of Venice progressed rapidly in the Church and soon after his grandfather's death he became a cardinal.'

Jack turned to the countess and looked at her. 'Does the name Cardinal Contarini ring a bell? *Think!'*

The countess shook her head. 'Sounds familiar, but ...'

Jack reached for the bottle and filled up the countess's glass. 'It should, because we both know him as His Holiness, Pope Pius XIII.'

Stunned silence.

'You can't be serious!' said the countess after a while, as the implications of what she had just heard began to sink in.

'What do you say, Signor Bonato?'

'Yes, Marco Contarini is Pope Pius XIII, the most illustrious member of the Alberti family,' said Bonato. 'He inherited Palazzo Alberti from his mother. He's the present owner, and I am looking after the palazzo for him.'

Palazzo da Baggio, Venice: the next morning

Bonato arrived unannounced at the Palazzo da Baggio the next morning with a large bouquet of flowers. He went to see the countess and thanked her for a wonderful evening. He also told her that he had thought carefully about what had been discussed the night before, and asked if he could see Jack.

The countess took him up to the terrace, where Jack was enjoying his first coffee of the day and the warmth of the morning sun caressing his face.

'We meet again, Signor Bonato,' said Jack, 'and so soon.'

If Jack was in any way surprised by Bonato's unexpected visit, he certainly didn't show it. Instead, he pointed to a basket of pastries and a coffee plunger on the table.

'Coffee?'

Bonato nodded.

'I can strongly recommend the pastries. Still warm. I think I'm falling in love with this city,' continued Jack.

'It gets into your blood. I couldn't imagine living anywhere else. I think it's the bells. Somehow, they keep the city's history alive, don't you think?'

'They do indeed. I know someone else who said something similar to me in Florence. There, it's the bells of Santa Maria del Fiore I find enchanting. Here, it's the *Marangona* with its beautiful, haunting tone, especially at midnight when it's quiet.'

'Ah, the wonderful bell in the campanile in the Piazza San Marco.'

Bonato sat down and helped himself to one of the pastries.

'Did you know that the *Marangona* is the only bell that survived the collapse of the tower in 1902?' continued Bonato. 'Originally, there were five.'

'I didn't know that.'

'They all had names and signalled specific events.'

'You don't say.'

'There was the *Maleficio*, with its sombre tone. It rang when a public

81

execution was about to take place. Then there was *La Nona*, which announced the ninth hour. The *La Trottiera* called magistrates to the Palazzo Ducale and the *Pregadi* announced meetings of the Senate. Simple and effective. But the most loved bell of all was the *Marangona*, which rang twice a day. At the beginning of the workday, and at the end. It's named after the *marangoni*, the carpenters. It was Alberti's favourite bell.'

'You are well informed.'

'I was a librarian – here, and in Padua – for almost forty years. All thanks to an early introduction to the wonderful world of books in the palazzo library, and an education sponsored by Alberti. As you can imagine, the library was a magical place for a young boy. And Alberti was like a magician who opened my eyes and my mind.'

'Ah, I know exactly what you mean. My eyes and my mind were opened in a provincial newspaper office in Brisbane. Until then, all I knew was how to muster cattle and sit around the campfire with Aboriginal drovers in outback Australia, listening to yarns.' Jack paused and looked at Bonato sitting opposite. 'What brings you here this early in the morning, Signor Bonato? Just to thank the countess for her hospitality, or was there perhaps more?'

'I barely slept last night. Two things kept me awake: the suicide note you mentioned, and the Treblinka records you called "the last remaining voice of thousands, reaching out from the mass grave to be heard". I couldn't help thinking about that. I think you are right; the two are definitely related. The fact that the letter you mentioned and the Treblinka records were next to the suicide note, make that a compelling conclusion.'

'I agree,' said Jack.

'You asked me last night if I could perhaps shed some light on the suicide note: "*I am so sorry, my darling.*"'

Jack nodded.

'I believe I can. How relevant it all is, or how helpful, will be for you to judge.'

'Understood.'

'This is further complicated by the fact that most of it is based on rumours, and snippets of information gleaned from my grandmother over the years. And as we both know, rumours can be unreliable and misleading. And so can grandmothers,' added Bonato, smiling.

'They can, but they can also act as a disguise for the truth. It's all to do with Isabella Contarini, isn't it?' said Jack, trying to help Bonato, who was clearly struggling with something.

'You are right. It has. You are very perceptive, Mr Rogan. And those rumours touch on something that happened well before I was born, the passage of time adding more uncertainty to it all.'

Bonato suddenly looked more relaxed.

'The reason I've decided to tell you this has to do with Alberti's character,' continued Bonato.

'In what way?'

'As you can imagine, I knew him very well, perhaps better than most. He was a man who thought very carefully about everything he did. Being spontaneous or impulsive or, God forbid, irrational, just wasn't in his nature. The fact that he left a suicide note is significant. The fact that he left that tin with the letter and the Treblinka records we talked about next to it, is poignant. I believe he wanted *both* to be found. And, of course, on top of it all is the date.'

'What date?'

'The date of his suicide.'

'Is that significant?'

'It sure is. To me, it is perhaps the most telling aspect of it all.'

'How come?'

'Because everything here is connected. It all became clear to me last night. You may laugh at this, but do you know when?'

'Tell me.'

'When I heard the *Maragona* toll at midnight. It was like a voice from the past trying to tell me something. Strange, don't you think? Alberti and I often listened to that bell together ...'

'I wish Tristan could hear this,' said Jack.

'Why?'

83

'Because he wouldn't find this strange at all. He would even have a name for it.'

'What name?'

'Destiny.'

Bonato smiled. 'I think that says it all. Alberti was trying to tell us something in death that he couldn't say, or face, in life. The fact that Padre Angelis took both the suicide note and the tin with him and made them disappear, thwarted that. That's why I've decided to help you find them, if you can. Does this make sense?'

'It does. We often do things for reasons that are difficult to explain—'

'Jack would call it following your breadcrumbs of destiny,' said Tristan, who had been listening by the open door for a while. He put a fresh plunger of coffee next to the empty one, and pulled up a chair. 'I couldn't sleep last night, either. In fact, I've been expecting you, Signor Bonato. I knew you would come. Now, let's see where these breadcrumbs take us, shall we?'

On the way to Rome: 9 August 2019

Jack had spent most of the night going over his notes in an effort to make sense of the Herzl story so far. He had also prepared a timeline, which was always helpful to put people and events into proper perspective. The information provided by Bonato regarding Alberti's suicide note was not only intriguing, but, he had to admit, it answered a number of questions and filled in a puzzling gap: it provided a possible explanation for the suicide, but didn't explain why the Treblinka letter was sent to Alberti in the first place. The connection between Alberti and the Herzl letter was still unclear, and without knowing what the letter contained, major gaps in the story remained. Then Tristan came up with an idea, and the idea pointed to Rome.

Jack decided to catch an early train. He loved trains and preferred train travel to flying. To him, it was a wonderful way to relax and experience at least a little of the countryside. He settled back into his comfortable seat and watched the outskirts of Venice glide silently past as the train gathered speed and turned south on its way to Rome.

Jack wanted to be in Rome by lunchtime. To get an appointment with the Dean of the College of Cardinals at short notice was never easy, but once Jack had managed to be put through to Cardinal Borromeo, everything fell into place. Jack had a special relationship with the cardinal, and His Eminence didn't even ask why Jack wanted to see him urgently. Instead, he said he would inform the Swiss Guards at the Apostolic Palace of Jack's imminent arrival and instruct them to bring him straight to his office. All Jack would say was that the matter did concern the Holy Father.

Jack opened his briefcase, pulled out his notebook, and opened it.

'Well, what do you think?' asked Tristan, who was sitting opposite and watching Jack carefully. 'You have been at it all night.'

'We are on our way to Rome, aren't we?'

'We are, but you didn't answer my question.'

'It's an interesting theory.'

'It's more than that, admit it. It fits the facts, and pulls together everything we've found out so far. Padre Angelis is the key here. I have no doubt about it. He was present at all the crucial events. Not only present, he was an *active participant*. Let's not forget that.'

Jack put down his notebook and glanced at Tristan.

'All right. Let's have a closer look,' he said. 'There are two key events here, and we have precise dates for both. According to Bonato, the first event of significance took place on 21 June 1924, and we know that the second occurred exactly forty-one years later, on 21 June 1965.'

'Correct,' said Tristan. 'And, of course, that's not the only link, is it?'

'No. Both events took place in the *same room* in the Palazzo Alberti, and Angelis was present on both occasions. Quite bizarre, really.'

'One was a birth, the other a death,' said Tristan. 'The alpha, and the omega. The beginning, and the end.'

'If Bonato's right and Alberti's daughter, Isabella – then at a tender age of seventeen – gave birth to a baby boy on 21 June 1924, in secret, that would explain a lot. Bonato's grandmother, a midwife, delivered the baby, and both Alberti – Isabella's father – and Angelis, the village priest, were present.'

'It was a very difficult birth,' said Tristan. 'Isabella almost died and was told that the baby had been stillborn, which apparently wasn't the case. The baby was alive and well.'

'The birth was hushed up and the baby disappeared. Bonato's grandmother was sworn to secrecy, and the baby was never spoken of again,' said Jack. 'Obviously, this too is significant.'

'Assume for the moment that Bonato is right again, and the baby wasn't stillborn but was taken away and disappeared. That could explain the suicide note – *"I'm so sorry, my darling"* – couldn't it?' suggested Tristan.

'It could. Guilt, remorse, regret, but it doesn't tell us what happened to the baby.'

'No, but let's have a look at what followed. Two years later, Isabella married Dominic Contarini, the son of a wealthy merchant from Padua,' said Tristan. 'It was an arranged marriage – Dominic was much older – but obviously it wouldn't have eventuated if the young bride had an illegitimate child bouncing on her knees, right?'

'Almost certainly not. The newlywed couple came to live with Alberti in the family mansion in Arquà Petrarca, which Alberti gave them as a wedding present. Three years later, they had a son, Marco—'

'As we heard, destined for great things from the very beginning,' said Jack.

'It would seem so. Now, let's have a closer look at Padre Angelis,' said Tristan. 'Alberti and Angelis are very close. Angelis, a Jesuit, has been the village priest at Arquà Petrarca since 1914. He takes great interest in Marco from the very beginning, becomes his mentor and oversees his education. This relationship never changes. It only becomes stronger. Guided by Angelis, Marco enters first the seminary, then the Church, and advances rapidly. By the time Alberti commits suicide, Marco is the Patriarch of Venice. He is only thirty-six.'

'All right, this could explain why Angelis, with Armantini's help, covered up the suicide, which almost certainly would have harmed Marco's illustrious career. In the Catholic Church, scandal is the big no-no. Angelis was an ambitious man. I would suggest he would have done almost anything to avoid a scandal, and protect his protégée's career.'

'Hm, you could be right. In fact, what happened soon after Alberti died, actually supports that. Apparently, Marco gave a spectacular eulogy at his grandfather's funeral, which, incidentally, was held in the Church of San Giorgio Maggiore—'

'Same place where Lorenza's funeral service was held, officiated by none other than Cardinal Borromeo, whom we are going to see,' interjected Tristan, a touch of sadness in his voice. 'Strange wheels within wheels rolling towards us out of the past, don't you think?'

Jack nodded. 'Remember what Bonato told us? Marco's eulogy not only inspired the mourners, who turned out by the hundreds, but impressed the Church Fathers in Rome. Apparently, Marco was a charismatic speaker, with fire in his belly. The Patriarch of Venice was called to Rome soon after the funeral, and was made a cardinal four years later. He was only forty. We also know that Angelis went to Rome as well. Let's find out why. I believe that will answer many of our questions. Don't forget, he took not only the suicide note with him, he took the Treblinka letter and records as well. Both disappeared.'

Tristan paused and looked pensively out the window. 'If they still exist, I believe we'll find them in Rome,' he said. 'I'm sure of it!'

'Because all roads lead to Rome?' teased Jack. 'Look, we are already in Florence. How time flies when you are trying to reconstruct the past.'

Vatican: 9 August 2019

The traffic in Rome was chaotic as usual, and hailing a taxi at Termini Station was not for the faint-hearted. There was no queue as such, only much shouting, pushing and shoving, where elbows and high heels were used as weapons and suitcases as shields. All that mattered was to snare that taxi, and claim victory – Roman style.

'Welcome to Rome,' said Jack.

'We should have called Bartolli. She could have picked us up with her Vespa,' joked Tristan.

'Only room for one on the back of a Vespa, mate.'

'Bugger! Here comes one – quick!' said Tristan and launched himself at an arriving taxi, narrowly beating a middle-aged businessman using a rolled-up newspaper as a club, to the back door. 'I only hope that getting into the Vatican will be a little easier.'

'It will be, trust me. Swiss Guards tolerate no nonsense.'

'I hope so.'

Once Jack had identified himself, the Swiss Guard in his outrageous uniform escorted Jack and Tristan up the stairs to Cardinal Borromeo's office in the Apostolic Palace, where the pope worked and lived. Because the pope had been in poor health for some time and relied heavily on Cardinal Borromeo, an office had been set up for Borromeo – the Dean of the College of Cardinals – next to the pontiff's study.

Furnished with antiques and precious paintings, Borromeo's office was palatial, the huge Biedermeier desk from Austria dominating the room like an intimidating symbol of learning and power.

Cardinal Borromeo, an influential prince of the Church, greeted Jack and Tristan like old friends. Their unusual relationship went back several years to 2016. The pope had been very ill at the time and was only saved from certain death by a revolutionary drug discovered by Professor Alexandra Delacroix, a Nobel laureate, at the Gordon Institute in Sydney. Jack had been instrumental in locating a famous Ottoman manuscript in the Vatican Secret Archive – *al-Qanun* – which quite sensationally had played a major role in saving the pontiff's life. Jack had written about it in his book *Professor K: The Final Quest*, which had become a *New York Times* bestseller. Then, a short time later, Jack had discovered a precious Russian musical score hidden inside a Russian icon, the famous Kazanskaya Bogomater, a gift from The Blue Army of Our Lady of Fatima, hanging in the pope's study. This extraordinary discovery culminated in a papal visit to Russia, and the return of the holy icon to the Alexander Nevsky Cathedral in Yekaterinburg in 2017. Jack had written a book about that too – *The Lost Symphony* – which also became an international bestseller. Jack was therefore no stranger to the Vatican.

'What brings you here, gentlemen?' asked Borromeo.

'An extraordinary story, Eminence,' said Jack, choosing his words carefully. 'The voice of murdered multitudes reaching out of the past to be heard.'

'How intriguing,' said Borromeo. 'And this involves His Holiness? You said so on the phone.'

'Yes, we believe it does, and how that came about is a separate story all by itself. A fascinating one. And it is that story which brings us to you, because we believe the answers are to be found right here in the Vatican.'

'In what way? Can you tell me more?' said Borromeo, frowning.

'Certainly, Eminence,' said Jack. 'It all began with a letter—'

'*Another* letter?' said Borromeo, smiling. 'Just like Empress Alexandra's letter in the lost symphony affair?'

Jack nodded. 'As Eminence will see in a moment, the two matters have a lot in common – surprisingly so,' he said.

Over the next half hour Jack gave a brief outline of the Herzl story, what had been discovered so far, and what was still missing and why. He told Borromeo everything except the part about Isabella's confinement in 1924, because he wanted to be absolutely certain that this part of the story was accurate, and had a bearing on the Treblinka letter. The sensitive nature and far-reaching consequences of that, still somewhat speculative information, demanded it.

'So, it all comes down to this, Eminence,' said Jack. 'We believe that Padre Angelis and the Treblinka letter are the key here. Tristan is convinced that the answers we are looking for are once again to be found right here, possibly hidden somewhere in the Vatican Secret Archive—'

'Because he could hear the whisper of angels?' said Borromeo, a sparkle in his eyes, 'Showing him the way?' He was by no means mocking Tristan. On the contrary, he was well aware of Tristan's extraordinary powers and took them seriously.

'Something like that.'

'And you are just following your breadcrumbs of destiny, I suppose?' said Borromeo, referring to the well-known phrase used often by Jack in his books.

'Yes, Eminence. And strangely enough, they brought me to you. We need your help—'

'Regarding information about Padre Angelis and his relationship with His Holiness after he became a cardinal?'

'Yes, and before. Padre Angelis knew His Holiness since childhood ...'

'Hm. Well, gentlemen, you are in luck.'

'In what way?'

'His Holiness has authorised the writing of a biography. He said that working on a biography while one is still alive makes more sense than having one created later, when one has left the world of the living. He believes that everything looks different when examined in the rear-view mirror.'

Jack smiled. Madame Petrova had used almost the same words during their first meeting.

'Work on the biography is in progress right now,' continued Borromeo. 'His Holiness is collaborating closely with the author. He is helping with the research and guiding him into the hidden corners of his life. For the sake of accuracy, you understand. That's where you may come in, if you find what you are looking for. What do you think?'

'Could be, Eminence,' said Jack.

'His Holiness wants to be remembered as the "Peace Pope".'

'And with good reason. His accomplishments are extraordinary in that regard,' said Jack.

'In no small manner due to you. It was only after he recovered from his grave illness that His Holiness could travel to the US and address the United Nations and Congress, remember? And we now know the consequences of that, especially in the Middle East, don't we? But back to the biography. I think you should talk to the author. If anyone can help you with your enquiries, it's him. A very learned man, and brilliant researcher.'

'He's here in the Vatican?'

'Yes.'

'Excellent. I would appreciate an introduction, if that could be arranged,' said Jack.

Borromeo looked at Jack, smiling. 'No need,' he said. 'You already know him and have worked with him.'

'I *have*?' said Jack, surprised.

'You have. In the *al-Qanun* search right here in the Vatican Library, as I recall it.'

'*Father Connor*?' Jack looked stunned.

'None other. His Holiness was very impressed with his work. After all, he was the one who located *al-Qanun* buried in the Vatican Secret Archive, right? And you wrote an entire book about it: *Professor K: The Final Quest.*'

'That's right,' said Jack. 'And we found *al-Qanun* just in time. Without that, well ...'

'The biography may have had to be written after His Holiness's death,' said Borromeo. 'I'll tell Father Connor you're here and arrange a meeting. I'm sure he will be delighted to see you. Before you go, there's one more thing you should know,' said Borromeo, turning serious. 'But please keep this to yourselves for the time being.'

'His Holiness is dying,' said Tristan softly.

'How did you know? But then again, I shouldn't be surprised. Unfortunately, the old disease has returned – with a vengeance.' Borromeo shook his head. 'Only this time, no new drugs or exotic cures can save His Holiness, I'm afraid. Old age. The doctors are unanimous.'

'How long?' asked Jack.

'A few days, at best.'

With that, Borromeo stood up, signalling the end of the meeting. 'Please keep me informed, but do keep in mind that there isn't much time. I hope you find what you are looking for. My secretary will take you to Father Connor now.'

In the Vatican Secret Archive: 9 August 2019

The Vatican Secret Archive was a depository of a vast body of state papers, accounting records, correspondence and a host of other documents, such as the personal papers of notable church officials, accumulated by the Catholic Church over the centuries. All carefully stored and meticulously catalogued. Until his death or resignation, the Sovereign of Vatican City – the Pontiff – had ownership of all the documents in the Vatican Secret Archive. Upon his death, ownership passed to his successor. Access to the material was strictly controlled, and permission was only granted for research purposes to scholars after careful scrutiny. Otherwise, the archive was strictly off limits to outsiders.

Father Connor, a Jesuit scholar Jack had worked with before, was sitting at his designated desk in the Vatican Secret Archive, when Cardinal Borromeo's secretary tapped him on the shoulder. Connor took off his glasses and looked up.

'Someone here to meet you,' said the secretary. He pointed to the door, and withdrew.

'Jack? *You?* Here?' said Connor. He stood up, walked over to Jack and embraced him.

'What are you doing here? Trying to find another secret text buried in the mists of time to save a life?'

'Not quite, but close,' said Jack and pointed to someone standing behind him. 'Look, there's someone else here to see you.'

Tristan? What on earth brings you two here?' said Connor, surprised, and shook Tristan's hand. 'Must be important. I am so sorry about Lorenza,' said Connor. 'We were all devastated. Come, take a seat and tell me what brings you here. They don't let just anybody in here, you know. You must have already been vetted by Cardinal Borromeo, who keeps a close eye on the Secret Archive, otherwise you wouldn't be here.'

'You're right,' said Jack. He pulled his notebook out of his briefcase, and put it on the desk in front of him. With Connor, it was always best to come straight to the point. And besides, time was precious.

'Let's cut to the chase,' said Jack. 'What Tristan and I are investigating concerns His Holiness, and could be relevant to what you are working on right now.'

'His biography?' asked Connor.

'Yes. And if we are right, and you can help us fill in the gaps, the material could have – how will I put this? – far-reaching consequences.' By linking the Herzl letter to the pope, Jack realised he would have Connor's undivided attention.

'Seriously?'

'Yes, but we are still missing a few vital pieces of information to pull it all together. And if anyone can help us do that, you can. Especially in this place, because we believe if what we are looking for still exists, it's most likely in here.'

'All right. Tell me,' said Connor, his curiosity aroused.

Jack opened his notebook and looked at Connor. 'You won't be disappointed, promise!'

Dinner at Armando al Pantheon, Rome: 10 August 2019

As soon as Jack stepped into the crowded, wood-panelled restaurant and was shown to his table, he felt instantly at ease. Just like last time. He smiled as he remembered his first meeting with Professor Bartolli, the sophisticated criminal psychologist with the fearsome reputation, whose court appearances were legendary, and performances under cross-examination formidable, instilling fear in those brave enough to question her opinions and findings. He had met the professor in connection with the sensational Maurice Landru case the year before, and they had hit it off right from the beginning.

Jack ordered some olives and a bottle of 2007 Illuminati Ilico Riserva Montepulciano d'Abruzzo he knew his guest would enjoy, and then sat back, soaking up the bustling, rustic atmosphere. He had almost finished his second glass of wine when Professor Bartolli, looking a little flustered, walked in and waved as soon as she saw Jack sitting at a table facing the door.

Jack waved back and watched Bartolli, a tall, striking woman with a prominent Roman nose and wide-set green eyes that didn't seem to stop smiling, walk towards him.

'A phone call out of the blue, and a dinner invitation to one of my favourite restaurants,' said Bartolli. 'Must be my lucky day.'

Bartolli kissed Jack on his cheeks, took off her leather jacket and sat down.

'No violin case to push under the table tonight?' asked Jack, a teasing sparkle in his eyes.

'It isn't Friday. No rehearsal. What brings you to Rome?'

On the last occasion, Bartolli, who played in a chamber orchestra in her spare time, had come straight from rehearsal. 'A long story, but a fascinating one,' said Jack.

'How surprising. Last time it was a serial killer, seven gruesome murders with half the police forces of Europe chasing the elusive culprit. You almost got killed, and then wrote a book about it that became a bestseller: *The Death Mask Murders*. Have I missed something?'

'No, that's fairly accurate. Is this a complaint?'

'Certainly not. I enjoyed the journey.'

'That's a relief!' said Jack, putting his hand on his heart.

'Is this perhaps something similar?' asked Bartolli, tying back her long, curly, dark-blonde hair with an elastic band she retrieved from her wrist.

'No. Quite different, in fact. It's about—'

Bartolli held up her hand. 'Let's order first. I'm starving.'

Food first. Of course, thought Jack. After all, this was Italy.

'Good idea,' he said, grinning. 'Go ahead and order for both of us. Like last time.'

Jack reached for the bottle and filled up Bartolli's glass. 'I'm in charge of the wine, you do the food; remember?'

'Abbastanza giusto – how do you say? – fair enough. Mother sends her regards. She was disappointed you didn't come for dinner at our place instead of coming here. She wanted to cook something special for you.' Bartolli shook her head. 'I can't imagine why, but you have her wrapped around your little finger.'

'Next time, promise. I need your undivided attention.'

'You mean without teenage daughters talking about boyfriends, a dog who thinks he's in charge, and a fussing mother?'

'That's a little harsh, but yes, I need your professional opinion and advice. You'll see why in a moment.'

'Sounds fascinating, especially coming from you.' Bartolli sat back, reached for her glass and looked expectantly at Jack. 'Let's hear it.'

Realising that time was of the essence, Jack gave a brief, point-by-point, almost clinical account of the Postmaster of Treblinka, his Ballroom of Hope, and the Herzl letter, all before *primi piatti* – the first course – was served, and food took over.

Then, before the second course – *secondi piatti* – arrived, he outlined what he and Tristan had been able to find out during their visit to Arquà Petrarca, their meeting with Bonato and what followed. He just made it before Saltimbocca alla Romana was served and Bartolli tucked in with gusto. If Jack thought she might be losing interest in the story, he was gravely mistaken. Bartolli had been listening carefully to every word, and was analysing the facts while her tastebuds began to dance to the mouth-watering tune of tender veal with prosciutto and sage, cooked in white wine.

At least I'll have a little more time before dessert, thought Jack, and tucked in as well. As a storyteller, he had intentionally saved up the best for last. The punchline was always the highlight – and he certainly had the mother of all punchlines ready to put on the table. And it all had to do with the Vatican Secret Archive, and what Father Connor had found earlier that day.

In the Vatican Secret Archive: 10 August, afternoon

After meeting Father Connor in the Vatican Secret Archive, Jack and Tristan had spent half the night and the entire next day looking for some reference or entry mentioning Father Angelis. All that they had to go by was his arrival in Rome soon after Alberti died, and he was recalled to the Vatican. That was in 1966.

They had all but given up, when Connor spotted an obscure entry in the electronic archive catalogue that was the only available guide through the 'Coliseum of hidden memories obscured by the march of time', as Connor liked to call the Vatican Secret Archive.

'Father Angelis was a Jesuit, right?' he asked.

'Yes. He never seemed to advance very far in the Church, but was nevertheless influential,' said Jack.

'Jesuits usually are. They like to keep to themselves, have their own agenda, and run their own race.'

Jack looked at Connor sitting opposite, amusement creasing the corners of his mouth and making his eyes sparkle.

'You don't say. You are a Jesuit, aren't you, Father?'

'Here, look at this,' said Connor, ignoring the remark, and turned his monitor around. 'We've been looking in the wrong places. Father Angelis died here in Rome in 1985, and his personal papers are stored right here with the Jesuits. They have their own section. A separate archive—'

'Secrets within secrets?' ventured Tristan.

'Something like that,' said Connor. 'I'll arrange for the records to be sent up. It shouldn't take long. I know everybody who works around here by now.'

'Not much, is it?' said Jack, looking at the small metal storage box one of the clerks had put on the table. 'Angelis was eighty-seven when he died, and this is his legacy? A small box? The detritus of a long life?'

'Let's look inside first, shall we,' said Connor, 'before we jump to conclusions? It's not the quantity that counts, but the quality. Don't forget, this is a Jesuit we are talking about. If I remember correctly, you once told me that $E = mc^2$ fits on the back of a postage stamp.'

'Einstein's theory of relativity,' said Jack. 'Correct.'

'That changed how we see the world,' continued Connor. 'Let's see if what's in here can perhaps do something similar, shall we?' He pushed the box across the table towards Jack. 'You open it. After all, it's your story.'

Slowly, Jack opened the metal container, his hands shaking. When he looked inside, a broad smile spread across his face as he lifted a small, rusty tin out of the container, and placed it carefully on the table.

* * *

'I know you can tell a good story, Jack,' said Bartolli, 'but could you please come to the point before curiosity kills me?'

'Well, all the answers we'd been looking for were in that tin. The letter Herzl delivered in 1946 and handed to Alberti, and the Treblinka records that were attached to it, were all there. And most important of all, Alberti's suicide note was there as well. Angelis had kept it all. All the missing pieces were there and neatly fell into place. Just waiting—'

'To be discovered by someone like you?'

Jack shrugged.

'Can you tell me more about those missing pieces?'

'I can do one better. I can *show* you.' Jack reached into his pocket, slowly pulled out a piece of paper, and placed it on the table in front of Bartolli like a magician pulling an unexpected surprise out of a hat to wow the audience.

'This is a copy of the letter written by Django Santi and handed to Herzl, the Postmaster of Treblinka, by his son, Anibal, a few days after Django was sent to the gas chamber.'

Bartolli put on her glasses and began to read:

Treblinka, 1943

Gentile Signor Alberti

I am writing to you from a place of unimaginable horror: Treblinka, just outside Warsaw, where the Germans are secretly killing hundreds of thousands.

I am turning to you now in the hour of our greatest need, because we have a special bond: Anibal. I have never stopped loving Isabella, but I believe the end is approaching. You are an honourable man who will not abandon or forget us, of that I'm sure. Whether you decide to tell Isabella about our fate, is up to you. You will know what's best.

I am the voivode now, after Menowin, my father, was killed by the Germans. Our clan was trying to cross into Hungary when we ran into a German patrol. They shot our horses, burned our wagons and transported us to a concentration camp. That was more than a year ago. Until then we had managed to avoid the Germans, which was in no small way due to my father's leadership. But our luck ran out and he was shot while trying to persuade the German officer to let us go.

We are beyond help here and most of our clan has already been killed, including women and children. Anibal and I are the last two survivors, but not for long, I fear. Only memories will remain and it is those memories, and the memories of thousands who have suffered the same fate, I am entrusting into your hands. Please make sure they are not forgotten and the world learns about the atrocities committed here, and takes note.

During our time here in the death camp, I have secretly prepared an account of what is happening here. I have tried to be as accurate as possible and it is this precious record I am sending you now. Please use it wisely because it may be the only surviving voice of thousands hoping to be heard.

Anibal believes he has found a way to get this letter to you, unlikely as that sounds. He has become a strong, clever young man. He would have made a good voivode. You can be proud of him, just as I am.

Please don't abandon us. Don't abandon the memory of your grandson.

I am begging you.

Django Santi

Scribbled in a different handwriting at the bottom of the letter was a note from Anibal Santi to Alberti:

Time is running out. My father, Django, was taken to the gas chamber yesterday. I'm sure I will follow him soon.

There is an underground postal network here in the camp run by a brave man, the 'Postmaster of Treblinka'. He has promised to deliver this letter to you.

I hope he succeeds, because if he doesn't, we will surely be forgotten. Forever.

Anibal Santi

Visibly affected by what she had just read, Bartolli took off her glasses and looked at Jack with moist eyes, and blinked away tears. 'This is all very moving, and the story about the Postmaster of Treblinka is fascinating, but what does it all *mean?* I completely understand your interest in the Treblinka records, but why are you so interested in Alberti?'

'You put your finger right on it, no doubt just like you do so effectively in court.'

'Yes. So?'

Jack reached for his wine glass, and took his time before replying. He was savouring the moment, pleased to be able to share it with someone like Bartolli, who would understand the potential impact of the letter and its consequences. And most important of all, she would understand his dilemma.

'I am interested in Alberti because of who he is.'

'*Is?* I don't understand. He's dead, right?'

'Yes, of course. This letter is like a pebble thrown into a still pond, and we both know what follows when that happens.'

'Yes, of course, ripples, but you're speaking in riddles. Ripples in whose pond? *Who was Alberti?*'

'Alberti was the father of Isabella you just read about. Isabella had two sons: Anibal, who wrote the note at the bottom here, and Marco. The sons had different fathers. Django Santi, who wrote this letter, was the father of Anibal, who was born in 1924 when Isabella was just seventeen—'

'This is all about a family tree, I can see that,' interrupted Bartolli, sounding a little frustrated and impatient, 'but why is this so important to *you*?'

'Because of the other son. Isabella married Alfonso Contarini two years after she gave birth to Anibal, and we now know what happened to him. Isabella and Alfonso had a son, Marco, who entered the priesthood and became the Patriarch of Venice at the young age of thirty-six. Can you see where this is heading?'

'Not yet, but go on.'

'Marco Contarini became a cardinal four years after his grandfather, Claudio Alberti, committed suicide ...'

'*It can't be*, surely!' said Bartolli, a stunned look on her face as recognition dawned.

'Oh yes, it is. This is the cardinal who later became His Holiness, Pope Pius XIII, the current pontiff who is very ill and about to die. That's why I am so interested in Alberti and this particular family tree. Well, one tragic branch of it.'

Jack reached across the table and put his hand on Bartolli's. 'And that's why I need your help.'

'In what way?'

'To solve a moral dilemma.'

'Oh?'

'It has been left up to me to make a critical decision here. Urgently, because time is running out.'

'What kind of decision?'

'Is it morally justifiable to tell a dying man at the end of a long, illustrious life about something that could change the way he perceives his past, his family, and those who were closest to him? Is it justifiable to tell that man that his mother had a secret lover when she was only seventeen and had an illegitimate child, a boy? How do you tell that man that he had a half-brother who ended up in a German concentration camp and died a horrible death, together with his father, who documented the atrocities committed in the death camp? How do you tell that man that his grandfather killed himself out of guilt and remorse to do with all this, and left a suicide note obviously meant for his daughter – His Holiness's mother? What should be done with those precious eyewitness accounts of what happened in Treblinka? The voice of thousands reaching out of the mass grave to be heard? In short, Francesca, what's the right thing to do here?'

'I see. Are you absolutely certain that your interpretation of what you have unearthed is correct? Are we talking about facts here, or perhaps speculation, at least in part?'

'A valid question. I've asked myself the same thing, but the answer is an unequivocal *yes;* we are talking about facts.'

'How can you be so sure?'

'Because of the other thing we found in the Jesuit storage box.'

'Oh? What was that?'

'Father Angelis's diary. While a number of critical entries are cryptic and some of them are written in some kind of code, especially names, when looked at in light of what we now know from other sources, especially the letter I just showed you, there is no doubt about the veracity of our interpretation. We are dealing with facts here, not speculation. Certainly, as far as the key elements of the story are concerned.'

'I understand. Quite a decision to make. I can see that.'

'You have been in situations of extreme stress before, where every word counts, and anything can happen with lives at stake, and whole generations potentially affected. I know the kind of cases you've been involved in.'

'Hm. Ah, here come our *dolci*,' said Bartolli, welcoming the distraction that would give her time to consider her answer. 'I couldn't decide, so I ordered two different desserts: Cassata Siciliana, and Tartufo di Pizzo. We can share.'

Sweets to the rescue, thought Jack, smiling, *Italian style.* 'I trust your judgement,' said Jack.

'With the dessert?'

'No, with everything.'

Papal apartments, Apostolic Palace, Vatican: 11 August 2019

Cardinal Borromeo had arranged an early morning meeting in his study with Jack, Tristan and Father Connor.

'His Holiness had a bad night,' said Borromeo. 'I just spoke to Professor Montessori, his physician. Not long now. Strangely, as so often happens with approaching death, while the body is weak and failing, the mind is strong and lucid. This is the case with His Holiness right now. I have told him that you are here, Jack, and would like to see him – alone. He was delighted and is ready for you. What I didn't tell him was that you may have something important to tell him. That will be up to you. Have you made a decision?'

'I have, Eminence. It wasn't easy …'

'I can imagine.'

'I consulted a friend last night, which was very helpful, and discussed the matter with Tristan here and Father Connor. They have once again examined all the available material overnight, especially the Herzl letter and the Angelis diary. We all agree that the facts are now unambiguous and supported by convincing written evidence. We are also in agreement that His Holiness should be told about everything we have discovered. The truth must never be hidden or denied, whatever the cost, personal or otherwise. The Treblinka records are a good example.'

Borromeo nodded. 'Very well. It was the decision I expected.'

'The only thing I would like to leave up to His Holiness is this,' continued Jack. 'I believe it should be up to him to decide how much, if any, of all this should be included in his biography and if so, how. The same applies to the Treblinka records. They are a very personal account of what happened in the death camp, written by the father of his half-brother. Both died in Treblinka.'

Borromeo stood up. 'I understand. I will take you to him now. It's time, come.'

Jack stood up as well and looked at Tristan. Their eyes locked, as both realised this was another moment of destiny. As Jack walked past

Tristan, Tristan grabbed his hand and squeezed it in a gesture of understanding and love that words alone could not express.

The short distance from Borromeo's study to the pope's bedchamber felt like one of the longest walks Jack had ever taken.

Borromeo stopped in front on the door and looked at Jack. 'You will find the words. Trust yourself.' With that, he opened the door and stepped aside.

As Jack entered the room, the bells of St Peter's Basilica were ringing. It was eight am. The tall windows of the large room were open, inviting the rays of the morning sun inside, like fingers of hope reaching out to the dying patient. The pope's bed had been turned around to face the windows so that he could see the cupola of St Peter's.

For a moment Jack stood quite still, and listened to the bells.

'Come closer so that I can see you,' said the pope, his voice surprisingly strong. 'Aren't they beautiful? There are six of them: the *Campanone*, the *Campanoncino*, the *Campana della Rota*, the *Campana della Predica*, the *Ave Maria* and the *Campanella*. My friends sound a little sad today. I think they know ...'

Jack walked over to the bed, his heart beating like a drum, and looked at the pope. The gaunt face and sunken eyes barely resembled the man who only a short time ago had travelled to Russia to return the holy icon to where it belonged. The pope extended his bony right hand. As Jack bent down to kiss the Fisherman's Ring, the pope placed his left hand on Jack's head. It was a gesture of friendship and blessing. 'I have been expecting you,' said the pope.

'You have, Holiness?' said Jack, surprised. 'How come?'

'Do you really think Tristan is the only one who can hear the whisper of angels?' The pope pointed to a chair next to his bed. 'Come, sit close to me. Isn't it a beautiful morning?'

'It sure is, Holiness. I have something to tell you ...'

'To be expected from a storyteller like you. Remember the holy icon, the Kazanskaya Bogomater, hanging on the wall in this very room? Just over there by the window.'

'I do.'

'And what a story you told me about that, and look where it took us. Amazing. Is this perhaps something similar?'

'Not quite.'

'Oh? What's it about?'

'This story is about you, Holiness.'

'About *me*?' said the pontiff. 'At this late hour?'

'Destiny may listen to the bells, but it ignores the hour.'

'How right you are. Now, what is it you wanted to tell me?'

An hour later, one of the Swiss guards escorted Jack back to Borromeo's study.

'How did it go?' asked Borromeo.

For a moment, Jack stood motionless in the doorway – tears in his eyes – and looked at something in the distance only he could see. Tristan stood up and walked over to Jack. He had never seen Jack so emotional before. The meeting with the pope had clearly affected him deeply. 'How are you?' he said.

Jack looked at Borromeo watching him. 'Could we please go into St Peter's, like last time when Lorenza met His Holiness?' he said instead.

'Sure, I'll take you.'

'Why do you want to go there now?' asked Tristan.

'I want to show you something.'

'*Me?*'

'Yes. Could we perhaps all go, and that includes you, Father Connor, and I'll tell you what happened,' said Jack.

'Of course,' said Borromeo. 'Follow me. As you know, there's a shortcut we can take.'

'Like last time?' said Jack.

'Yes. Just like last time.'

They entered the basilica through a side door close to the high altar. Tristan stopped and looked at the stunning columns of the famous St Peter's Baldachin directly under the huge dome. Bernini's masterpiece – an inspired blend of sculptures and architecture – stood directly above St Peter's tomb. The imposing structure reaching towards Michelangelo's breathtaking dome was a visual link between the basilica's enormous size and the human scale of the papal altar beneath the canopy.

'Why have you brought us here, Jack?' asked Tristan.

'His Holiness suggested it. He asked how you were coping with Lorenza's death.'

'What did you tell him?'

'Hm ... I came here with Lorenza after she met His Holiness in 2016. She was cooking for him in the Vatican kitchen and served him an Ottoman dish based on an ancient recipe that saved his life. Under the supervision of a Nobel laureate—'

'Alexandra Delacroix.'

'Yes, but you know about all that. On that occasion, His Holiness wanted to meet Lorenza, alone. After the meeting she was very emotional and asked to come here. Apparently, His Holiness had suggested it.'

'As he did just now?'

'Yes. He asked me to bring you here.'

'Why?'

'He said if you listen to the whisper of angels, you will find out.' Jack pointed to a small side altar. 'Lorenza walked over to that little altar there, and lit two candles. One for her mother, and one for her brother. If you light one for Lorenza and listen, then perhaps ...'

Tristan nodded and walked over to a little wrought-iron stand full of flickering candles. Slowly, he lit a candle and then walked over to the altar and just stood there, his head bowed in silence.

Borromeo turned to Jack standing next to him. 'Following those breadcrumbs again?' he said softly.

'Yes, only this time I had a very special guide to show me the way.'

'I can see God's hand in all this,' said Borromeo, 'just like last time we stood here and watched Lorenza kneeling in front of that very same altar. Strange, isn't it?'

'Quite. Let's hope it has the same effect.'

'It will; you'll see. How did His Holiness—?'

'Take it all? Calmly and with grace. He's an extraordinary man.'

'Did you show him the letter and the suicide note?' asked Connor.

'I did. He read them carefully.'

'And? What about the biography?'

'He asked me to write a detailed account of everything that happened and add it to the biography you are working on. He specifically told me to leave nothing out.'

'Amazing,' said Connor, shaking his head.

'I hope you don't mind.'

Mind? Not at all! On the contrary, it will be a fitting addition that will characterise and define his biography: honesty, courage and authenticity. Quite rare in biographies of illustrious people who only like to be remembered for the glamorous bits.'

'What about the Treblinka records?' asked Borromeo. 'Did you talk about that too?'

'We did. His Holiness had a close look at those as well, and read them carefully. He seemed very affected by it all. Not surprising when you think of it. It's all very confronting.'

'And did he say what he had in mind?' asked Borromeo, aware that time was running out.

'He didn't elaborate, but said that he would tell *you*—'

Just then, Tristan turned slowly around and came walking towards Jack. As he came closer, Jack noticed something remarkable: an expression of peace on Tristan's face he hadn't seen before.

'We'll wait for you at the side entrance over there and take you back when you're ready,' said Borromeo quietly, and withdrew with Connor.

As soon as they were alone, Tristan embraced Jack. 'You were right,' he whispered. 'This is a special place. She took away my grief.'

'Who? Lorenza?'

'I was with her, just now. Right here. The wounds have healed. The grief has gone!'

Jack smiled as he remembered Lorenza using almost the same words to describe her experience at the altar. 'That's why I brought you here.'

Clementine Hall, Apostolic Palace, Vatican: five days later

Jack stood in the historical Clementine Hall in the Vatican's Apostolic Palace, and watched dignitaries from around the world pay their respects to a much-loved pope, Pius XIII, who was lying in repose. It had been five days since Jack's visit to the pope's bedchamber.

The death of a pope is rigorously ruled by an ancient ritual and involves a number of formal steps that must be followed:

The *Camerlengo,* the pope's chamberlain, is in charge and is responsible for making sure that all formalities are strictly observed.

First, standing next to the pope's body, he calls out the pope's birth name three times. If there is no response, he must obtain a death certificate and then notify the cardinal vicar of the diocese of Rome. Only then can the pope be declared dead and the black smoke, the *fumata nera,* be released through the famous chimney of the Sistine Chapel, to tell the world that the pope is dead.

This marks the beginning of the *interregnum,* a period without a pope that is also governed by strict rules, culminating in *conclave,* the traditional process of electing a new pope. This takes place usually after a nine-day period of mourning called *novemdiales.*

'He looks so serene,' Jack said to Father Connor, who stood next to him.

'He died peacefully. I was there. He knew he made a difference.'

'He sure did, right down to his last breath.'

'Yes, you're right. One of the last things he did was to instruct Cardinal Borromeo about what should happen to the Treblinka records you gave him earlier that day. Not bad for a sick man about to die, when you think of it. He was lucid and in control to the very end.'

Connor turned to face Jack. 'And, of course, His Holiness had already told you earlier what he wanted you to do with the Alberti suicide note.'

'Yes, he did. He was quite specific about that.'

'And you will do as he asked?'

'Of course.'

111

'It's quite an ask.'

'It is, but I owe him that.'

'I have something for you, Jack.' Connor reached into his tunic and pulled out a large envelope.

'What's that?'

'The final draft of the Holy Father's biography. Thank you for getting your part done so promptly.'

'It was no problem. I had everything at my fingertips. I hope it did the job.'

'It did more than that. You spoke from the heart, and that always shows and makes a difference. Especially with a subject as sensitive as this.'

Jack nodded. 'I'm glad you liked my little contribution. What happens now?'

'It will be published very quickly. Obviously, there's a lot of interest in the late pope's life right now. As you can see, he was – *is* – very popular. He wanted to be remembered as the "Peace Pope", and this biography will certainly help in that regard. It clearly sets out not only his life, but his extraordinary accomplishments as well, many of which are not generally known.'

'What about you? Where to from here?'

'I'm just a simple Jesuit. I do what I'm told.'

Jack looked at Connor, raised an eyebrow and smiled. 'So was Father Angelis ...'

'No, he was a *kingmaker*,' said Connor.

Jack looked at the pope lying peacefully on a bier only a few metres away. He looked regal and impressive even in death, with a red cape around his shoulders and a white bishop's mitre on his head, the long, papal silver crucifix tucked under one arm.

'I have a feeling our paths will cross again, Father,' said Jack.

'I hope so,' said Connor, and handed Jack the thick envelope with the late pope's biography inside. 'This is for you.'

Yad Vashem, Jerusalem: three months later

Surrounded by dignitaries and armed security guards, Jack stood in front of Yad Vashem. He was waiting for the arrival of the pope. *Not long now*, he thought. *He should be here soon.*

Jack had learned that Yad Vashem, the famous Holocaust memorial in Jerusalem, was established in 1953 on the western slopes of Mount Herzl. It is Israel's official memorial to the victims of the *Shoah*, the Holocaust. The name, Yad Vashem – literally 'a memorial and a name' – is taken from a verse in the Book of Isaiah and is based on a concept of establishing a memorial for murdered Jews who have no-one to carry on their name after death.

'It's wonderful that His Holiness should make this his first overseas trip of his pontificate, don't you think?' said Rabbi Stein, who looked very formidable in his Hasidic attire: a dark three-piece suit and a black hat made of rabbit fur. At Jack's invitation, he had flown in from Prague earlier that day to participate in the much-anticipated ceremony.

'It is, but you know why, don't you? He's fulfilling a promise made to his predecessor.'

'An honourable man.'

'He is that, and a consummate diplomat and negotiator. This should help with the peace process here, which is, of course, the other main reason for his visit. He will continue the agenda of Pope Pius XIII, and try to reignite peace negotiations if possible.'

Shortly after the death of Pope Pius XIII and a relatively short conclave, Cardinal Borromeo was elected pope. He took the name Gregory XVII.

'I still can't believe this is happening,' said Kun, who had arrived from Budapest the day before.

'It was Pope Pius's idea. He arranged it all on his deathbed. He wanted you involved. I was with him just hours before he died.'

'Before we go inside, I want to say something. Look around you, Jack,' said Kun. 'This is Yad Vashem, the world-famous Holocaust memorial, and we are delivering the Postmaster of Treblinka's letter to its final destination. This is history.'

'Everything around here is.'

'And you made it all possible and for that, I thank you.'

'We are all but instruments of destiny and fate,' said Jack.

'That we are, and this is certainly a moment of destiny, don't you think?' said Stein.

'It sure is,' replied Jack and looked at his watch. 'I was told the presentation ceremony will take place in the Hall of Names.'

'Most appropriate. Many say that the Hall of Names is the heart of this memorial because it specifically commemorates the six million murdered Jews of the Holocaust. The way it's designed is particularly pertinent and moving,' said Stein.

'In what way?' asked Kun. 'This is my first visit.'

'The hall consists of two cones. One is ten metres high, with an identical cone below hewn out of virgin rock with water at the bottom. The idea behind the design is as simple as it is effective. Displayed on the upper, dome-like cone are hundreds of photographs of victims, together with testimonial fragments documenting the atrocities committed in the death camps. This display is reflected in the water at the bottom of the cone carved out of the rock. This reflection commemorates victims who remain unknown, but not forgotten.'

'Like those from Treblinka we are about to honour today?' said Kun.

Stein nodded.

'Here they come now. Look!' said Jack, pointing to a procession of black cars approaching the memorial.

As soon as the cars stopped and were surrounded by security guards, the pope got out and was met by the chairman of the memorial, who then escorted the pontiff and his entourage to the entrance of the huge memorial complex, with its many symbolic sculptures and exhibits, and splendid views over Jerusalem.

As the pope approached the entrance, he saw Jack standing behind a group of security guards. He stopped and walked over to Jack. 'I'm glad you could make it,' said the pope and extended his hand.

'Your Holiness, may I present Rabbi Stein, and Sandor Kun, David Herzl's son,' said Jack, introducing the two men standing next to him.

'Please come with me, gentlemen. After all, you are very much part of why we are here, and what we are about to do.'

The security guards stepped aside and let Jack, Stein and Herzl join the pope's entourage and follow the pontiff inside.

After a brief introduction by the chairman in the stunning Hall of Names, the pontiff stepped forward and made a short, moving speech, in which he explained the significance of what was about to happen, and how it came about.

'We are all very privileged to have Sandor Kun – The Postmaster of Treblinka's son – present here today to deliver his father's letter to its final destination: right here, where it belongs.'

With that, the pontiff turned to Father Connor standing next to him and held out his hand. Connor, now the pope's secretary, handed him the rusty tin he had recently found in the Vatican Secret Archive. Because the pontiff not only controls the archive but actually owns all it contains, he is free to deal with all of it as he sees fit.

'Mr Kun, would you please step forward,' said the pope as cameras began to roll all around him, transmitting the solemn moment to the world.

Barely able to hold back the tears, Kun stepped forward and bowed his head as the pope handed him the tin. Then he turned slowly around and held it up, pointing it at the hundreds of faces looking down on him from above.

'After seventy-four years, the Postmaster of Treblinka's letter has finally arrived,' he said. Barely able to see because of the tears streaming down his gaunt face, Kun turned towards the chairman, handed him the tin, and then slowly returned to his place next to Jack. Deeply moved, Jack put his arm around him and held him tight.

As the pope walked past Jack on his way out, he stopped. 'When are you planning to do it?' he asked.

'As soon as I get back to Venice.'

'Please let Father Connor know when it's done.'

'I certainly will, Holiness,' said Jack and bowed his head.

The pope nodded, raised his right hand and made the sign of the cross before following the chairman out of the hall.

Cimitero di San Michele, Venice: three days later

'Everything's ready. Taxi's here; let's go,' said Jack and headed for the palazzo entrance leading to the pontoon facing the Canal Grande, where the water taxis usually tied up when delivering house guests.

It had rained during the night and a dense fog hovered over Venice like a shroud, giving the facades of the palazzos along the canal an ethereal, ghostlike appearance.

'Have you got everything?' asked the countess.

Jack pointed to the bag in his hand. 'I do.' He realised that the trip to the island cemetery would be an emotional one, especially for Tristan, because Lorenza was buried there in the da Baggio family vault.

Because visibility was poor, progress was slow. The man controlling the boat had to carefully feel his way along the busy waterways past San Giorgio Maggiore, the church where Cardinal Borromeo, now Pope Gregory XVII, had officiated over Lorenza's funeral.

Married by one pope and buried by another, thought Jack as the taxi passed the beautiful church, and he remembered the black funeral gondola with Lorenza's coffin slowly disappearing in the mist on its way to the very same island they were about to visit.

'Almost there,' said the driver as the fog parted to reveal a small island almost completely enclosed by a high wall.

Jack pointed to a church with a white Istrian stone facade dominating the water's edge. 'San Michele in Isola,' he said. 'Our destination.'

Jack walked over to the priest waiting at the entrance and introduced himself.

'Everything's ready,' said the priest, sounding displeased. To open a family vault inside a church was a serious matter, whatever the reason. But when instructions come from high up in the Vatican, one does as one's told, and the instructions to open the Contarini family vault came from about as high up as it gets – from the pope's personal secretary.

117

The priest pointed to a side altar. 'The Contarini family crypt is just below that altar over there. As you can see, the workers have already lifted the marble slab.'

'Thank you,' said Jack. 'I will be the one going down.'

Jack opened his bag, pulled out a small marble urn and looked at Tristan and the countess watching him. 'Well, this is it. The end of a long journey.'

'Can you show us?' said the countess.

'Sure.' Jack opened the lid of the beautiful urn, took out a small, neatly folded piece of paper, and handed it to the countess.

I'm so sorry, my darling,' read the countess, her eyes misting over. 'A father's last words to his daughter. So sad.'

'Words written in great pain and distress, but never delivered, until now,' said Jack and put the piece of paper back into the urn. 'This is what Pope Pius wanted. This is what he asked me to do once the Treblinka records had been delivered to Yad Vashem. Place an urn, with the suicide note inside, on top of his mother's coffin in the family crypt. His Holiness isn't buried here, of course. He's buried inside three coffins in the crypt under St Peter's Basilica, known as the Vatican Grottoes.'

'Three?' said the countess.

'Yes. The innermost coffin, which contains his body, is made of cypress to show that the pope was an ordinary man. The next one is a hermetically sealed zinc coffin, which was placed inside an oak coffin, which was then interred under a marble slab.'

'What happened to his ring?' asked Tristan.

'According to tradition, the Ring of the Fisherman is ceremonially destroyed with a hammer by the *Camerlengo*, the papal chamberlain, in the presence of cardinals. This is done to avoid forgery of documents during the *interregnum* after the pope's death and before a new one is elected.'

'Fascinating.'

'Are you ready?' asked the priest and handed Jack a torch.

'I am,' said Jack and began to climb down the narrow set of marble stairs leading to the dark crypt below.

Because there were a number of coffins in the crypt, it took Jack a couple of minutes to find Isabella Contarini's bronze coffin. For a moment he stood in front of it in silence. Then he carefully placed the small urn on top of the heavy lid, and stepped back. Mother, and the son she didn't know had lived, could now both rest in peace. And so could Isabella's father, because Jack was certain that she would forgive him for what he had done, so that his tortured soul could finally find peace.

On the way back, sunshine had banished the morning fog and the gloom that had hovered over the city had lifted. And so had Jack's spirits after he had kept his promise. Enjoying the fresh air and salty sea spray hitting his face, Jack turned to the countess standing next to him.

'I have an announcement to make,' he said, a broad grin spreading across his face.

'Oh-oh,' said the countess. 'Do you know anything about this, Tristan?'

'No. I have no idea what this is all about.'

'All right, Jack, let's have it.'

Enjoying the moment, Jack took his time before replying. He watched the water taxi turn into the Grand Canal and overtake a vaporetto full of tourists taking photographs.

'In a way, what I'm about to tell you is connected to the Postmaster of Treblinka saga we have just concluded. More specifically, it has to do with the Alberti family. Any ideas?'

'Is this turning into a quiz?' asked the countess, rolling her eyes.

'No. I'm just curious to see how well you know me. Tristan?'

'You *haven't!*' said Tristan, almost losing his balance.

'I haven't *what?*' said Jack, laughing.

'You *have!* I can see it on your face! You can't keep a bloody secret.'

'Would someone please tell me what's going on?' said the countess. 'You two can be so exasperating.'

'The incorrigible rascal here has bought the Alberti palazzo, haven't you, Jack?'

    'Tell me you haven't!' said the countess.

    'Why, don't you want me as your neighbour?'

MORE BOOKS BY THE AUTHOR

The Jack Rogan Mysteries Series Starter Library
The Empress Holds the Key
The Disappearance of Anna Popov
The Hidden Genes of Professor K
Professor K: The Final Quest
The Curious Case of the Missing Head
The Lost Symphony
The Death Mask Murders
The Jack Rogan Mysteries Series Box Set Books 1–5

THE JACK ROGAN MYSTERIES SERIES
STARTER LIBRARY

So, what exactly is a STARTER LIBRARY? I hear you ask. Well, it's a way to introduce myself and what I do, to new readers, and create interest in my writing. How? By providing little insights into my world, and the creative process involved in becoming an international thriller writer.

The Starter Library consists of four short books:
1. ***Letters from The Attic*** – a delightful collection of auto-biographical short stories;
2. ***The Forgotten Painting*** – a multi-award-winning Jack Rogan novella, providing insights into Jack Rogan's character and background;
3. ***The Kimberley Secret*** – a novella delving into Jack Rogan's earlier life;
4. ***Jack Rogan Mysteries Main Characters*** – a glossary which provides some exciting background stories and insights into the main characters featured in the series, and acts as an aid mémoire to place and follow the many characters featured in the series.

The Starter Library is available right now, and can be downloaded for FREE by following this link: https://gabrielfarago.com.au/starter-library2/

Please share this with your friends and encourage them to download the Starter Library.

In 2013, I released my first adventure thriller –
The Empress Holds the Key.

THE EMPRESS HOLDS THE KEY

A disturbing, edge-of-your-seat historical mystery thriller

Jack Rogan Mysteries Book 1

Dark secrets. A holy relic. An ancient quest reignited.

Jack Rogan's discovery of a disturbing old photograph in the ashes of a rural Australian cottage draws the journalist into a dangerous hunt with the ultimate stakes.

The tangled web of clues – including hoards of Nazi gold, hidden Swiss bank accounts, and a long-forgotten mass grave – implicate wealthy banker Sir Eric Newman and lead to a trial with shocking revelations.

A holy relic mysteriously erased from the pages of history is suddenly up for grabs to those willing to sacrifice everything to find it. Rogan and his companions must follow historical leads through ancient Egypt to the Crusades and the Knights Templar, to uncover a secret that could destroy the foundations of the Catholic Church and challenge the history of Christianity itself.

Will Rogan succeed in bringing the dark mystery into the light, or will the powers desperately working against him ensure the ancient truths remain buried forever?

The Empress Holds the Key
is now available in ebook and paperback

Encouraged by the reception of *The Empress Holds the Key*, I released
my next thriller –*The Disappearance of Anna Popov* – in 2014.

THE DISAPPEARANCE OF ANNA POPOV

A dark, page-turning psychological thriller

Jack Rogan Mysteries Book 2

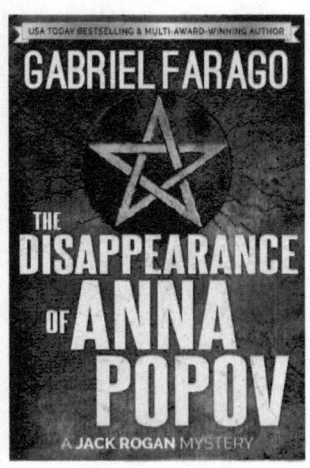

**A mysterious disappearance. An outlaw bikie gang. One dangerous
investigation.**

Journalist Jack Rogan cannot resist a good mystery. When he stumbles
across a hidden clue about the tragic disappearance of two girls from
Alice Springs years earlier, he's determined to investigate.

Joining forces with his New York literary agent, a retired
Aboriginal police officer, and Cassandra, an enigmatic psychic, Rogan
enters the dark and dangerous world of an outlaw bikie gang ruled by
an evil master.

Entangled in a web of violence, superstition and fear, Rogan and
his friends follow the trail of the missing girls into the remote Dream-
time-wilderness of outback Australia, where they face their greatest
challenge yet.

Cassandra has a secret agenda of her own and uses her occult powers to conjure up an epic showdown where the stakes are high, and the loser faces death and oblivion.

Will Rogan succeed in finding the truth, or will the forces of evil prevail, causing untold misery and destroying even more lives?

The Disappearance of Anna Popov
is now available in ebook and paperback

My next book, *The Hidden Genes of Professor K*, was released in 2016.

THE HIDDEN GENES OF PROFESSOR K

A dark, disturbing and nail-biting medical thriller

Jack Rogan Mysteries Book 3

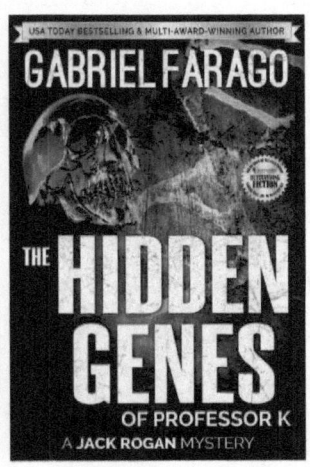

A medical breakthrough. A greedy pharmaceutical magnate. A brutal double-murder. One tangled web of lies.

World-renowned scientist Professor K is close to a groundbreaking discovery. He's also dying. With his last breath, he anoints Dr Alexandra Delacroix his successor and pleads with her to carry on his work.

But powerful forces will stop at nothing to possess the research, unwittingly plunging Delacroix into a treacherous world of unbridled ambition and greed.

Desperate and alone, she turns to celebrated author and journalist, Jack Rogan.

Rogan must help Delacroix, while also assisting famous rock star Isis in the seemingly unrelated investigation into the brutal murder of her parents.

With the support of Isis's resourceful PA, a former police officer, a tireless campaigner for the destitute and forgotten, and a gifted boy with psychic powers, Rogan exposes a complex web of fiercely guarded secrets and heinous crimes of the past that can ruin them all and change history.

Will the dreams of a visionary scientist with the power to change the future of medicine fall into the wrong hands, or will his genius benefit mankind and prevent untold misery and suffering for generations to come?

Gold Medal Winner in the Fiction – Thriller – Medical Category
Readers' Favorite 2019 International Book Awards Contest

The Hidden Genes of Professor K
is now available in ebook and paperback

My next book, *Professor K: The Final Quest*,
was released in October 2018.

PROFESSOR K: THE FINAL QUEST

An action-packed historical medical mystery

Jack Rogan Mysteries Book 4

**A desperate plea from the Vatican. A kidnapped chef. An ambitious
mob boss. One perilous game.**

When Professor Alexandra Delacroix is called in to find a cure for the
dying pope, she follows clues left by her mentor and friend, the late
Professor K, which lead her on a breathtaking search through
historical secrets, some of them deadly.

Her old friend Jack Rogan must step in to assist while he's also
searching for kidnapped Top Chef Europe winner Lorenza da Baggio.

He joins forces with his young friend and gifted psychic, Tristan; a
dedicated Mafia-hunting prosecutor; a fearless young police officer;
and an enigmatic Egyptian detective on a perilous hunt for a notorious
IS terrorist.

Together, they stand off with the head of a powerful Mafia family in Florence and uncover a network of corruption and heinous crimes reaching to the very top.

Will Rogan and his friends succeed in finding Lorenza and curing the pope, or will the dark forces swirling around them prevail in their sinister plots?

Gold Medal Winner in the Fiction – Thriller – Medical genre!
2019 Readers' Favorite Annual Book Award Contest

Professor K: The Final Quest
is now available ebook and paperback

My fifth book, *The Curious Case of the Missing Head*,
was released in November 2019.

THE CURIOUS CASE OF THE MISSING HEAD

A gripping medical thriller

Jack Rogan Mysteries Book 5

**A headless body on a boat. An international conspiracy. Can Jack
survive a controversial scientific discovery?**

Esteemed Australian journalist Jack Rogan is on a mission to solve the
disappearance of his mother in the 1970s. But when a friend needs
help rescuing a kidnapped world-renowned astrophysicist, he doesn't
hesitate. Struggling with more questions than answers, his investigation
leads them aboard a hellish hospital ship, where instead of finding the
kidnap victim, he's confronted with a decapitated corpse.

As the search intensifies, Jack bumps up against diabolical cartels
with hidden agendas. And when his research reveals dubious
experiments, a criminal on death row, and a shocking revelation about
his mother's fate, he must uncover how it's all linked.

Can Jack unravel the twisted connections and catch the scientist's killer, or will the next obituary published be his own?

The Curious Case of the Missing Head is the fifth standalone novel in the page-turning *Jack Rogan Mysteries Series*. If you like meticulous theoretical science, exponential intensity and astonishing surprises, then you'll love Gabriel Farago's hair-raising medical thriller.

Gold Medal Winner in the Fiction – Thriller – Conspiracy Category
Readers' Favorite 2020 International Book Awards Contest

"Outstanding Thriller/Suspense" of 2020
Independent Author Network Book of the Year Awards

The Curious Case of the Missing Head
is now available ebook and paperback

My sixth book, *The Lost Symphony*, was released in November 2020.

THE LOST SYMPHONY

A historical mystery thriller

Jack Rogan Mysteries Book 6

A murdered tsarina. A lost musical masterpiece. A stolen Russian icon. Can Jack honour a promise made a long time ago, and solve an age-old mystery?
When acclaimed Australian journalist and author Jack Rogan inherits an old music box with a curious letter hidden inside, he decides to investigate. As he delves deeper into a murky past of secrets and violence, he soon discovers that he's not the only one interested in solving the puzzle.

Frieda Malenkova, a ruthless art dealer, and Victor Sokolov, a Russian billionaire with a dark past, will stop at nothing to achieve their deep desires and foil Jack's valiant struggle to uncover the truth.

Joining forces with Mademoiselle Darrieux, a flamboyant Paris socialite, and Claude Dupree, a retired French police officer, Jack enters a dangerous world of unbridled ambition, murder and greed, which threatens to destroy him.

On a perilous journey that takes him deep into Russia, Jack follows a tortuous path of discovery, disappointment and betrayal that brings him face to face with his destiny.

Will Jack unravel the hidden clues left behind by a desperate empress? Can he save the precious legacy of a genius before it's too late, and return a holy icon revered by generations to where it belongs?

The Lost Symphony is the sixth standalone novel in the page-turning Jack Rogan Mysteries Series. If you enjoy historical mysteries based on meticulous research, fascinating characters, and edge-of-your seat excitement, then you'll love Gabriel Farago's latest action-thriller.

Gold Medal Winner in the Fiction – Mystery – Historical Category
Readers' Favorite 2021 International Book Awards Contest

Award-Winning Finalist in the Fiction: Thriller/Adventure Category
The 2021 International Book Awards

The Lost Symphony
is now available in ebook and paperback

My seventh book, *The Death Mask Murders*,
was released in December 2021.

THE DEATH MASK MURDERS

A historical mystery crime thriller

Jack Rogan Mysteries Book 7

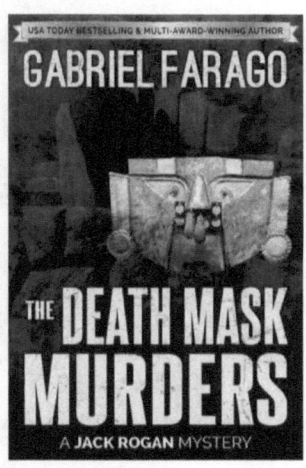

Seven brutal murders. A cursed Inca burial mask. A lost treasure. One deadly game.

When convicted killer Maurice Landru reaches out from a Paris prison and asks for help to prove his innocence, celebrated author Jack Rogan cannot resist. Drawn into a web of hidden clues pointing to an ancient mystery, Jack decides to investigate.

Joining forces with Francesca Bartolli, a glamorous criminal profiler; Mademoiselle Darrieux, an eccentric Paris socialite; and Claude Dupree, a retired French police officer, Jack enters a dangerous world of depraved cyber-gambling, where the stakes are high and the players will stop at nothing to satisfy their dark desires.

Following his 'breadcrumbs of destiny', Jack soon comes up against an evil genius who terminates his enemies without mercy and is prepared to risk all to win.

On a perilous journey littered with violence and death, Jack uncovers dark secrets of a murky past of ruthless conquistadors, bloodthirsty pirates and shipwrecked priests, all pointing to a fabulous treasure, waiting to be discovered.

Can Jack expose the mastermind behind the horrific murders and retrieve the legendary treasure before it falls into the wrong hands, or will the forces of darkness overwhelm him and destroy everything he believes in?

The Death Mask Murders is Book 7 in *The Jack Rogan Mysteries Series* for the thinking reader and culturally curious, and can also be enjoyed as a standalone novel.

The Death Mask Murders
is now available in ebook and paperback

JACK ROGAN MYSTERIES
BOX SET BOOKS 1-5

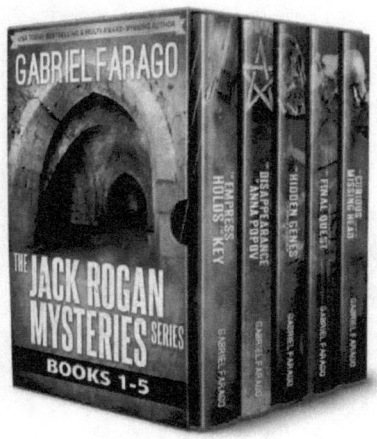

The Jack Rogan Mysteries Box Set
is now available in ebook

ABOUT THE AUTHOR

Gabriel Farago is the *USA TODAY* best-selling and multi-award-winning Australian author of *The Jack Rogan Mysteries Series* for the thinking reader.

As a lawyer with a passion for history and archaeology, Gabriel Farago had to wait many years before being able to pursue another passion – writing – in earnest. However, his love of books and storytelling started long before that.

'I remember as a young boy reading biographies and history books with a torch under the bed covers,' he recalls, 'and then writing stories about archaeologists and explorers the next day, instead of doing homework. While I regularly got into trouble for this, I believe we can only do well in our endeavours if we are passionate about the things we love. For me, writing has become a passion.'

Born in Budapest, Gabriel grew up in postwar Europe and, after fleeing Hungary with his parents during the Revolution in 1956, he went to school in Austria before arriving in Australia as a teenager. This allowed him to become multilingual and feel 'at home' in different countries and diverse cultures.

Shaped by a long legal career and experiences spanning several decades and continents, his is a mature voice that speaks in many tongues. Gabriel holds degrees in literature and law, speaks several languages and takes research and authenticity very seriously. Inquisitive by nature, he studied Egyptology and learned to read the hieroglyphs. He travels extensively and visits all of the locations mentioned in his books.

'I try to weave fact and fiction into a seamless storyline', he explains. 'By blurring the boundaries between the two, the reader is never quite sure where one ends, and the other begins. This is, of course, quite deliberate, as it creates the illusion of authenticity and reality in a work that is pure fiction. A successful work of fiction is a balancing act: reality must rub shoulders with imagination in a way that is both entertaining and plausible.'

Gabriel lives just outside Sydney, Australia, in the Blue Mountains, surrounded by a World Heritage National Park. 'The beauty and solitude of this unique environment,' he points out, 'gives me the inspiration and energy to weave my thoughts and ideas into stories that in turn, I sincerely hope, will entertain and inspire my readers.'

Gabriel Farago

Author's Note

I hope you enjoyed reading this book as much as I enjoyed writing it. I'd be very grateful if you'd post a short review on Amazon. Your support really does make a difference.

CONNECT WITH THE AUTHOR

Website
https://gabrielfarago.com.au/

Goodreads
https://www.goodreads.com/author/show/7435911.Gabriel_Farago

Facebook
https://www.facebook.com/GabrielFaragoAuthor

BookBub
https://www.bookbub.com/profile/gabriel-farago

Sign up for the author's New Releases mailing list and get a free copy of *The Forgotten Painting** novella, to find out where it all began ...

https://gabrielfarago.com.au/free-download-forgotten-painting/

* I'm delighted to tell you that *The Forgotten Painting* has just received two major literary awards in the US. It was awarded the Gold Medal by Readers' Favorite in the Short Stories and Novellas category and was named the 'Outstanding Novella' of 2018 by the Independent Author Network (IAN) Book of the Year Awards.